CW01082039

The Sacred Tor

The Talisman - Book III

The Sacred Tor

Michael Harling

iv

Lindenwald **LP** Press

To Mitch and Charlie
Without whom there would be no story.

Also by Michael Harling

The Postcards Trilogy
Postcards From Across the Pond
More Postcards From Across the Pond
Postcards From Ireland

The Talisman Series
The Magic Cloak
The Roman Villa

Finding Rachel Davenport

Chapter 1
July 2015

Mitch

The screen door slammed behind us.

"Is that you?" Mom shouted from the kitchen.

"No," Charlie called. "It's a burglar."

"Don't get smart with me, young man. How was ball practice?"

I kicked my sneakers off and tossed my glove onto the dining room table.

"Fine," I said.

Charlie put his shoes next to mine and dropped his glove on top of them. "Yeah, it was great. Mitch struck out."

"Only once. And I got three hits. One of them a triple."

"That's nice," Mom said. "Don't put your dirty gear on the table. I'm about to serve up lunch and I just cleaned it."

I snatched my glove off the table and brushed the grit onto the floor.

"Oh, and your grandfather sent you something. It's in the living room."

The blood drained from my face. I looked at Charlie. His eyes were wide. "Shit."

I nodded.

It could only mean one thing: we were meant to use

the cloak, yet again, and I had been sure that last time was the last time.

Two years ago, at the beginning of summer, Granddad sent us a cloak as a gift. And, as if that wasn't crazy enough, he told us it was magic. Naturally, we didn't believe him, but then the cloak took us on a strange adventure, a sort of hyper-realistic dream—a not altogether pleasant hyper-realistic dream. We knew it had to have been a dream because it couldn't possibly have been real. But then, last summer, he sent a second gift—two bags of replica coins—and the cloak took us on another hyper-realistic (not to mention painful and smelly) adventure-dream.

The memories of those dreams had faded over the months, but now they came back, sharp and clear, making me wonder if they had been dreams after all. A jumble of images exploded in my mind, threatening to overwhelm me. Then I realized someone was speaking.

"And wash your hands." It was Mom, still calling to us from the kitchen. "Now go see what Frank sent you," she continued, in an overly cheerful tone, "I'm curious to see what it is."

But I wasn't. I went upstairs to wash. In my room, as I changed my shirt, I looked at the cheap treasure chest box that Mom had locked the cloak in last year. I hadn't touched it since I'd put the cloak back in it and reattached the hinges, except to put it on a low table, just to get it off my dresser. In the months that followed, I had forgotten about it, never believing I would have to take it out again.

After I changed, I went back downstairs to find Charlie sitting in the living room, staring at a flat, square cardboard box.

"Shall we open it?" he asked as I sat next to him.

"We'll have to," I said.

Charlie nodded. "But, after last time … do you remember last time? I didn't, but now I do. Does that make sense?"

"Yeah," I said, "it's the same for me."

"All that stuff about closing the circles. I was sure that meant we were done with this."

"Maybe there's a bigger circle," I said, tapping the box with my foot. "What do you think it is?"

"Dunno. Looks like it could be a bicycle tire."

"Why would he send us something like that?"

"Why would he send us a cloak?"

A clink of plates came from the dining room.

"So, what have you got this year?" Mom called.

"And that's another thing," Charlie said, keeping his voice low. "First, she tried to keep the cloak from us. Then she locked up the coins, and the cloak. Why is she being so cool about this one?"

I started tearing tape off the box. "She thinks it's still locked up in that trunk. She's got no reason to be uncool about it."

Charlie helped me pull the flaps open. "Still, it seems weird. She was so angry at Granddad for running off to England that she wouldn't even let us have the gifts he sent. And now she's okay with it?"

We tore away the top and pulled the crumpled newspaper out. "Maybe she's over it."

Charlie huffed. "Mom? Get real."

"What have you got?"

I looked up as Mom came into the room. "We don't know yet."

"Shields," Charlie said, lifting two big discs out of the box. As he did, a piece of paper fluttered to the floor.

3

"Granddad's letter," I said, picking it up.

Mom knelt on the floor and inspected one of the discs. They were the same size, but coloured differently, made from wooden frames with material stretched over them. One was painted to look like wood with a big X of iron dividing it into quarters. The other also had an iron X painted on it, but it had alternating sections of blue and yellow.

"They're very detailed," Mom said. "They look almost real." She saw me reading the letter. "What does he say about them?"

"He says he's doing well," I said, "and wonders if we enjoyed the books he sent us for Christmas."

I'd received a set of books about someone called Alex Rider. He'd sent Charlie ones about a boy with the unlikely name of Artemis Fowl, that he hadn't read yet. I'd read all of them, hoping they might give a clue to what was going on, but they were just adventure books.

"If he'd send us an email address or tell us where he lives," Charlie said, "then we could tell him."

That was something Mom would usually have said, but she kept silent, and continued to stare at me with a smile frozen on her face.

"Seems he went back to the what-not shop that old man runs," I continued, scanning the letter. "This time the guy pointed him toward these Saxon shields."

Charlie held one of the shields like he was in battle. "Saxon? When were they around?"

"The Roman Era, and for some time after," I said, exhausting all the knowledge I had about them.

Charlie lowered his shield. "Roman era?"

"Yeah."

That was where we had ended up last time, and I

4

didn't want to go back again.

"They certainly look like something you can have fun with," Mom said.

Charlie dropped the shield back in the box. "Mom, we're fourteen, not five."

"Well, your grandfather seems to think you'll enjoy them."

Charlie sighed. "He would. Let's eat."

◆

Lunch was awkward, punctuated by forced laughter and fake smiles. I kept my head down and ate my egg salad sandwich and tomato soup, then went outside to sit on the back porch. A short time later, Charlie came out and sat with me.

"You're going to use the cloak tonight," he said.

I nodded. "I think we're supposed to."

Charlie glanced at the screen door to make sure Mom wasn't listening. "Can you still get at it?"

"Yeah. Far as I can tell, she hasn't touched the box since she locked it up. She still thinks it's secure."

"Then why's she acting so funny. She seems nervous."

"I don't know. Maybe Dad finally put his foot down."

Charlie rocked back in his chair. "Could be. She still hasn't forgiven Granddad, but keeping the shields away from us won't change anything. And it won't do any good. She can't lock them up like she did with the coins, they're too big."

"Good thing," I said, "because then she'd find out they're gone."

Then I had a sudden thought. What if she had looked in the box? She'd have discovered that the coins were missing. She would know I'd opened it. Would that make her realize keeping the gifts from us wasn't going to work, or would it make her more determined?

"You're going to want me to come with you," Charlie said, breaking into my thoughts.

"I think that's how it's supposed to happen."

"And if I don't agree, you'll just kidnap me, like last time."

"I'd rather not."

Charlie remained quiet for a few minutes. Then said, "Well, this is how it's going to be. I'll pack up some stuff, supplies like food and matches, so we don't have to wait while someone bangs two rocks together, and we can—"

"You know that won't work. Nothing comes with us except the gift, and our clothes."

"What's the point of going back in time if I can't bring anything with me?"

"I think that kinda is the point," I said. "Why go back in time if you're just going to bring the modern world with you? Just be glad our clothes come with us."

He kept quiet for a long time, so long that I decided to go back into the house. But he spoke as I stood up.

"What time?"

I looked at my watch. "It's one-forty-seven."

"No, what time are we going?"

I hadn't thought about that. "Well, last time it was about three o'clock. How about then? We can both stay awake. That will make it easier to fall asleep under the cloak. I'll come to your room—"

"No. I'm not going to sit up all night. Come to me when you're ready. I'll sleep in my clothes. Cover me up, and we'll do it." He looked up at me, his face more serious than I ever remember seeing it. "I don't want

6

this," he said. "I don't know what's going on, but it scares me."

"I feel the same, but …" I waved my hand toward the door, "… the shields."

He looked down. "Yeah," he said, nodding. "The shields."

I went inside. Mom was in the kitchen, so I went into the living room and cleaned up the box and packing material. Then I carried the shields upstairs to my room and stood them in a corner. They really were well made. If you stood back, they looked almost real. But when you held them, you realized how flimsy they were.

"We should get the cloak out now" Charlie, who appeared so suddenly beside me it made me jump, said.

"What for? We can't use it until tonight. I can take it out then."

"It will save time, and keep you from fumbling around in the middle of the night."

It made sense, but part of me wanted to put it off as long as possible. "I don't know."

"If Mom hasn't looked in the box for a year, she's not suddenly going to open it now, is she?"

I wasn't as certain about that as he was, but it seemed a risk worth taking.

"Watch the door," I said.

Charlie sat on the end of my bed, keeping an eye on the hallway. I went to the table, pulled it away from the wall and turned it around so I could see the hinges. My heart pounded as I got out my Swiss Army knife and began removing the screws. I got the first hinge off, then started on the second. Everything seemed surreal. Was it really going to happen again? Images from the other dream adventures flashed in my mind: the fear, the cold, the pain, the elation, the old man, Pendragon, Kayla. I removed the second hinge and realized I was breathing in short, sharp gasps.

"Quick," Charlie said, getting off the bed.

He came and stood by me. I lifted the lid, using the hasp on the front of the box as a hinge. I moved it slowly, not wanting to drop it, or let it flop open so Mom would hear.

"Take it," Charlie said, his voice edged with excitement.

I lifted the lid as far as I dared and looked, open-mouthed into the box.

Then Charlie looked. "Shit."

The box was empty.

Chapter 2

Charlie

It took us two days to find the cloak, because we could only search for it when Mom was out, and if it hadn't been for me, we wouldn't have found it at all.

After Mitch put the hinges back on the empty box, we tried to forget about it. Mitch stayed in his room to read, and I went outside to toss the ball up in the air so I could practice catching it. (It really sucks having a brother who'd rather read than play catch.) When Dad got home, we showed him the shields. At first, he was a little edgy, wondering if Mom was going to go mental again, but when she seemed okay with us having them, he relaxed. And I was no longer nervous about what Mom was up to because I already knew: she had obviously opened the box at some point, found that the coins were missing and realized we could get into it. So, she'd taken it. What she did with it, we had no idea. She might have burned it for all we knew.

But we didn't worry about that. Granddad had done his part by sending us some ridiculous gifts. Mom was happy, Dad was relieved, and we were content with the idea that we wouldn't have to go on another terrifying mind-trip. We felt like we were supposed to, like it was some sort of duty, but the cloak was gone, and we couldn't go without it and that wasn't our fault. So, as far as I was concerned, it was a win all around.

That night, however, I couldn't sleep. I laid awake, staring into the darkness, worrying, and I didn't know why. I laid awake until the full moon shone through my window, and then I watched the rectangle of light slowly slip across the floor. At some point, I realize that, if we had gone, we'd have been back by now, but only after spending days, or weeks or even months, living some horrific ordeal. Yet I couldn't shake the feeling that we were wrong to not go. It felt as if I was running for the school bus, only to find it already rolling away, down the hill and out of sight.

The next morning, I waited until Mom was out of the room, then told Mitch we had to find the cloak.

"We'll never find it," he said, not looking up from his cereal. "It could be anywhere. And if we didn't go last night, it might not even work."

"But we have to try," I said. I felt embarrassed, unable to explain the feeling I'd had the night before. "I think we were supposed to go last night, and just because we couldn't, that doesn't mean we shouldn't. We were supposed to be there, and we need to go."

Mitch finally looked at me. "I thought you didn't want to go."

"I don't, it's just …" I thought again of those long, dark hours. "We need to go."

Mitch shrugged. "Mom's going shopping later. We can look then."

We decided to go outside so Mom wouldn't think we were waiting around for her to leave. When she left, we went back in and began our search.

We started in the basement, looking under Dad's work bench, in the cabinets and the partitioned off room where the furnace was. There weren't many places to hide a cloak in, and it didn't look like she could have stuffed it into the furnace, so we went back upstairs.

The living room, kitchen and hall took a long time to search. There were so many places she could have concealed the cloak and we had to check all of them—inside the clothes bags that Dad kept his suits in, down the back of the sofa, in the cupboards, under the sink, in the closet under the stairs. After we had exhausted all possibilities and found nothing, and were on our way upstairs, we heard Mom's car pull into the driveway, so we ran down the stairs and into the back yard as Mom came through the front door.

It was a difficult afternoon, trying to act normal, as if we weren't concerned about the cloak at all. I spent another sleepless night trying, unsuccessfully, to shake the growing feeling of dread gnawing at my stomach, and early the next morning, me and Mitch went to hide in the woods next to our house.

We told Mom we were going to the ballpark, hoping she would leave for her usual Friday volunteer shift at the library. She mostly did go, but occasionally she wouldn't, remarking—as she picked up a book and sat in the sun on the back porch—"What are they going to do? Dock my pay?"

Leaving her alone was a gamble. The idea of having a day to herself might be too tempting to pass up. But if we hung around the house, she might wonder what we were up to, so we sat in the woods, hiding in the undergrowth, where we could see the house and would know when, or if, Mom left.

When nine o'clock came and went and Mom didn't leave, neither of us said anything. I didn't want to be the one to say we'd failed, and Mitch didn't, either, so we sat, and watched, and waited. At ten minutes after nine, Mom's car pulled out of the driveway and headed toward town. We ducked down as she passed the woods, watching her as she drove by.

"She's headed to the library, all right," I said. "She always wears that blouse when she goes. She thinks it makes her look professional. We're good for the next six hours."

Mitch nodded but kept his eye on Mom's car as it disappeared. "But why'd she leave so late?"

I shrugged and got to my feet. "Who cares. Better late than never. Let's go."

Since we'd already searched the basement and first floor, we went straight up the stairs. Mom wouldn't have hidden the cloak in my bedroom, or Mitch's, and there was nowhere to hide it in the bathroom, so that only left the hall closet, and her and Dad's room, which we were both hesitant to go into. Mitch said it felt like an invasion of privacy, but I was afraid we'd stumble upon Dad's porn stash, which I suppose is the same thing. In the end we had to because the cloak wasn't in the closet. We were extra careful in there, making sure Mom, or Dad, wouldn't know we'd been through their stuff. Fortunately, we didn't find any porn. Unfortunately, we didn't find the cloak, either.

We knew it wasn't in the loft even before we looked because Mom never goes up there, and when we pushed on the hatch, it was obvious it hadn't been opened in years. Still, we went up, and spent too long investigating some of our old games and digging through boxes of old clothes that Mom must have put up there ten years ago and then forgot about.

"I guess she's smarter than we are," Mitch said, after we came down from the loft and cleaned up the mess opening the hatch had made. We had returned to the living room and were sitting on the sofa, with the television turned off.

"Maybe she burned it," I said.

Mitch shook his head. "No, I don't see her doing that."

"Then where is it?"

Mitch didn't answer, he just did that staring into space thing he did when he was thinking hard.

"Where would you hide something you didn't want anyone to find?"

Now it was my turn to stare into space. "I dunno. Somewhere no one would think to look."

Mitch's eyes came back into focus. "Exactly."

I hated it when he got like this. "Meaning?"

"Where did we not think to look today?"

"Well, down here."

"Why?"

"Because we've already looked here."

"So, maybe this is where she put it."

"But she couldn't know—"

Mitch cut me off. He clearly thought he was onto something. "Think about it. Look how neat this place is."

"So?"

"Mom cleaned and straightened it, remember, after she got back from shopping, even though it was already clean. You know what a neat-freak she is. We probably moved something off-centre, or left the clothes in the closet hanging in the wrong order."

I finally got it. "She knew we'd been searching for it down here. And she knew we hadn't looked upstairs because, well, we'd have found it."

I jumped up, ready to start the search again.

"No," Mitch said. "Don't touch anything. She'll

13

know."

"Then how—"

"Slowly, methodically, and logically. She only spent ten minutes this morning re-hiding it. Where is the best place?"

"The closet."

I opened the door and we looked in. The coats and seldom-used suits, zipped inside their garment bags, were straight and evenly spaced, the hangers all facing the same way, not at all like we had left it after our search the day before. Carefully, I dug through to the back, where one of the garment bags looked heavy and bulky at the bottom. I took it out and held it up. Mitch unzipped it and our cloak spilled out.

We decided to not wait until the evening. We still had about an hour until Mom got home, so we had plenty of time to use the cloak and put it back (hopefully, just the way we had found it) without her even knowing.

We prepared ourselves by dressing in rugged clothing, then went to Mitch's room and laid down on his bed. We put the shields on our chests and Mitch covered us with the cloak.

"We need to go to sleep," Mitch said, not realizing I was struggling to stay awake. "There's a technique I read about. Take a deep breath, let it out slowly, and count down from eleven, to ten, to nine, and with each breath, feel yourself sinking down, down, down. Ready?"

I nodded.

"Breathe in, and out. Eleven. In and out. Ten …"

I don't know about Mitch, but I didn't make it to nine.

Chapter 3
September 1066

Mitch

I felt a nudge and opened my eyes. Dark. Something, or someone, was pushing against my forehead, and there was a weight on my chest that made it hard to breathe.

"Charlie?"

Another nudge. I pulled the cloak away from my face. And screamed.

It wasn't Charlie. It was a huge tongue and an enormous, wet nose leaking snot. I scrambled backward but found myself hemmed in by bushes and still pinned down by the strange weight on my chest. The cow—for that's what was nudging me—snorted and poked its head deeper into the bushes. It was a stocky beast, rust-coloured, with short legs that looked capable of trampling me to death.

"Go! Shoo!"

I struggled to sit up. The cloak fell away and the shield that had been weighing me down slid off my chest. The cow pulled its head out of the bushes and trotted away. Beside me, Charlie sat up.

"Whaaa!" he said, trying to look in every direction at once.

"A cow," I told him, struggling to control my breathing.

Charlie laughed. "If that's the most dangerous thing we see, we'll be lucky."

Together we crawled out from beneath the tangle of bushes, dragging the cloak and our shields—now larger, heavier and all too real—with us. We were on the edge of a grassy area bordered by low brush and crisscrossed with muddy paths. My cow had joined a few others (all the same size and colour, though some had horns) not far away. A couple of them looked at us with disinterest, then resumed grazing. The sky was cloudless and blue, and the air was warm, but the grass felt damp, telling me it was still morning. Beyond the pasture were fields, stands of small trees, and meadows, some enclosed by stone walls, others by rows of hedges. Nothing looked familiar. The first time, we had appeared in a ring of holly bushes, and last time it had been an orchard. Now, there was nothing but a landscape that looked, for want of a better word, tired. The fields were empty, the leaves on the trees, though still green, had a weary, limp look, and the bushes we had appeared under were brittle and brown. I took a deep breath. The air was fresh, carrying the scent of dry grass and wet cows.

Charlie, standing beside me, looked to the left, then the right. "Do you think this is the same place?"

"I don't know."

"When do you think this is?"

"I don't know."

"Do you know anything?"

The cows, especially the ones with horns, were beginning to take an interest in us.

"I know we should get out of this field."

Our shields were lying on the ground where we had left them, their colouring and designs looking like they

16

always had, but they were no longer toys. I picked mine up, slid my arm through the leather straps and gripped the handle. It was heavy, but well-balanced and easy to manoeuvre. The polished metal gleamed in the sun as—recalling the training I had received from Fergus's squires—I swung to the right and left, tilting the shield up and down, warding off imaginary blows. Then, using the longer strap, I slung it over my shoulder, so it hung comfortably on my back.

"It feels like it was made for me."

"I think it was," Charlie said, testing his own shield. "Now let's get out of here."

The bush we had appeared under looked remarkably like every other bush, so I stood guard while Charlie gathered enough stones to make a crude arrow. The ground was rock-hard, and we had to jump on the stones to press them deep enough into the soil so they wouldn't be disturbed. Then, as an extra measure, Charlie crawled back under the bush and scratched a circle into the ground with a stick.

When we finished, I folded the cloak so it would be easier to carry. Then we stepped cautiously into the meadow, keeping well away from the cows, to see if we could figure out where we were. This time, it was a clear day, so we at least had a rough idea which direction to head in.

"If that's east," I said, pointing to the sun, "and if we are in the same place as before, then just a little way to the west of us, there should be a path, and that should lead us to the Roman Road."

It wasn't hard to find. The pasture was bordered by a low stone wall and, when we climbed over it, we found a rutted, dirt track. Beyond that was a wooden shack with a grass roof and a muddy yard cluttered with strange implements I took to be farming tools. Scrawny chickens pecked among the debris and, from behind the shack, I heard the rhythmic thump of someone chopping wood.

"Let's go before someone sees us," Charlie said. "We don't know when we are, but whenever this is, we won't exactly blend in."

I looked down: sneakers, jeans, tee shirt and a light jacket I had put on because, even though it was hot at our house, we didn't know what the weather would be like where we were going. Add to that the shields slung on our backs and the cloak I was carrying, and we wouldn't be able to pass unnoticed at any time in history, even our own. So, we turned north and walked away, hoping no one would come out of the house, but realizing, with a rising sense of dread, that at some point, someone was going to see us.

It wasn't long before we found the road, which told us we were exactly where I thought we were, but it didn't tell us when, or what we should do.

We hid behind some bushes while a cart, pulled by a cow, went by. The cart—small and made of wood—rattled and creaked as the cow, led by a man wearing worn leather boots, loose pants and a shirt that hung to his knees, ambled past and disappeared.

"What was in the cart?" Charlie asked. "It wasn't turnips, was it?"

"I don't know," I said, "but that guy wasn't Roman, and the road is in bad condition, so we must be well beyond those days. Perhaps even beyond the age of Pendragon."

"So, what do we do?"

I considered for a moment. No matter where we went, we were sure to run into people, and they were sure to find us strange, but there was nothing to be done about that.

"Go to where Pendragon's house is," I said, "or was, or will be. Maybe we'll find a clue there."

We followed the road toward where Horsham should be, stepping over potholes and cow plops. When we got to the place where the Roman farm had been, and where Pendragon had told us the giants had lived, there was no trace left, confirming that, whenever this was, it was years beyond the age Pendragon had lived in.

We crossed a stream over the same stone bridge that had been there since Roman times, though it looked in need of repair, and passed more fields and stretches of woodland. A few people were out in the fields, but none looked our way. Then we saw another cart and driver heading toward us. We felt that jumping off the road and hiding would look more suspicious than just carrying on, so that's what we did. The man on the cart, which was drawn by a horse, clopped by and we kept walking, trying to avoid eye-contact. The man didn't stop or challenge us, but he did stare as he went by.

Closer to town, the air took on a heavy farmyard-mixed-with-backed-up-sewer smell, and we saw more people, and a lot more cows, some on the road, some in the fields. The further we went, the more the road deteriorated, eventually becoming more mud and muck than stones. We picked our way through it, trying to keep our sneakers from getting too muddy, yet trying to not look prissy doing it because the locals were just slogging through, not caring that they were up to their ankles in it.

Ahead of us, a stone building, framed with timber,

sat near a crossroad. Charlie pointed at it. "That looks familiar. Do you think that's the house called The Green Dragon?"

"Yes," I said, feeling suddenly optimistic, "so this must be Horsham. We need to take that crossroad going south."

We turned right and kept walking, and the people around us, although there were still only a few of them, kept staring. Some glanced furtively at us, while others openly gaped, their faces a mixture of curiosity and fear. We kept our heads down and walked as quickly as we could. To our surprise, no one challenged us. It wasn't long before we crossed the bridge, over what we now knew to be the River Arun, and found the path that led to where Pendragon's house had been.

What had been a wide, flat lane in Roman times was now a narrow, rutted path with brambles growing on either side. We walked single file, past tangles of bushes and low trees, where a neat row of stone houses had been, until I began to lose hope. Then I spotted a clearing ahead of us.

The brush thinned out and stopped at a low stone wall surrounding a cluttered yard. The wall was in need of repair and covered by weeds in some spots. There was an opening at the edge of the path that looked like it used to be a gateway. A walkway, made of flat rocks sunk into the ground, led to a small, stone house with a wood and mud addition that nearly doubled its size. Despite these changes, it was most certainly the house of Pendragon and his family and, hundreds of years before that, the slave quarters where Kayla and her mother had stayed.

Unlike when Pendragon live there, the windows were no longer holes in the wall; they were square, wood-lined and had shutters. And the roof, though still thatched, had a hole where smoke rose into the still air. The doorway, too, had a more finished appearance, featuring a solid wooden door that stood slightly ajar. A few scrawny chickens pecked and scratched around the yard but, otherwise, there was no sign of life.

We went through the entrance and walked cautiously up the pathway. When we were about halfway to the house, I called out. "Hell-o."

Charlie shrugged. "I guess no one's—"

The door burst open and two large dogs bounded into the yard, barking and snarling.

"Whoa!"

"Hey!"

There was no use in running away. They were nearly upon us, and I didn't want to expose my back. I held the cloak up. The first dog—a heavy, black brute—bit it, shaking his head and growling as he pulled me and the cloak forward. Charlie swung his shield in front of him and used it to fend off the smaller, brown dog. A second later, before I even began thinking about how to get away, a sharp command cut through the din and the dogs abruptly stopped.

Charlie and I backed away, still holding the cloak and shield in front of us. The dogs stayed where they were, their heads up, their eyes alert.

Then a young woman stepped through the doorway. She looked at us, and the dogs, and shouted again. The dogs dropped their heads, turned, and trotted into the house. I lowered the cloak, and Charlie slung his shield onto his back.

The woman came closer. She was young, dressed in a loose, white smock made of coarse fabric and a tan skirt that hung down to the tops of her leather shoes.

She had fair skin and her head was wrapped in a grey scarf that covered her hair. She came forward slowly, her eyes never leaving us. When she got to where the dogs had been, she stopped. Her mouth formed a perfect "O," but no sound came out.

"Um, hell-o," Charlie said. "We're sorry to disturb you, but we're looking for—"

"It is you," the woman said.

Now I looked surprised.

"Our friend, Pendragon used to live here," I said. "We're searching for him. Can you help?"

The woman turned white and looked so much like she was going to faint that I thought I should run to catch her in case she fell, but she appeared to be terrified of us, so I stayed where I was.

"Are you all right?" Charlie asked.

The woman nodded. "Then, the legends are true?"

"I ... um, we ... what legends?"

"You are the knights." She stepped forward slowly and put her hand out, pointing at the cloak. "You have come to save the Land."

Charlie looked down, scuffing his feet in the dirt. "I think maybe we're talking about a different—"

"Valiant knights, from the ancient times," the woman continued. "What they told me was true."

I looked at her hand, still pointing at the cloak. "That sounds ... I mean, I'm not sure ..."

The woman dropped to her knees, her head bowed, her hands clasped as if in prayer. "You are the travellers. These are perilous times. You have come to save us."

"Wait a minute," Charlie said. "We're just ..." He turned to me and leaned close. "I don't like this; it doesn't sound good."

I nodded and took a step back. It wasn't at all what I had expected, and she really did appear to have mistaken us for someone else. "This seems to be a bad time to visit," I said. "Maybe we'll come back later."

The woman looked up, alarmed. "Sires, oh please, forgive my rudeness. Come into the house for rest and drink." She stood, her arms out, beckoning us with shaking hands. Her blue eyes shone with moisture. "Don't go," she pleaded. "I am Hilde, my husband is Aelric, descendant of Pendragon. His son, Edric, our future, lies sleeping in the house. For our sake, for the sake of this village, for the sake of the Land, you must not go."

Chapter 4

Charlie

We followed the woman to the house. At the open doorway, she paused and, with her head still bowed, waited for us to go in first. The dogs, lying by a fire in the centre of the room, jumped to their feet but stayed where they were. Hilde said something to them, and they trotted toward us, but without the look of murder in their eyes. Me and Mitch backed away as they came near, but they didn't even glance at us. They just kept going, through the door and out into the yard. I let out the breath I had been holding and looked around.

When Kayla had lived there, the room was bright and colourful, lit by oil lamps and the sun shining through the windows. When Pendragon lived there, it had looked like a cave. Now it was something in between. The walls were still dark, but there were three windows, making the interior a little brighter. The fireplace was still just a pit in the middle of the floor, but the air was more breathable because of a hole cut in the peak of the thatched roof, which allowed most of the smoke to escape. It was an improvement, but they obviously hadn't yet figured out what a chimney was for. The floor was packed earth with something that looked like cattail reeds scattered over it.

"Come, sires" she said. "Sit by the fire."

It wasn't much of a fire, just a heap of glowing coals that, as in Pendragon's day, had a metal frame over it, supporting a black pot hanging from a chain. I wondered if it was the same pot, then wondered where she expected us to sit. There was a small cabinet near one wall, a flat work surface covered with dishes, some shelves laden with clay jars, buckets, heaps of firewood, clumps of limp vegetables hanging from the ceiling, a broom, of the type favoured by witches, leaning in one corner, but no chairs. In the back of the room was the same table we had sat at with Garberend, Aisley and Pendragon, with the same benches next to it, but they looked too heavy to drag to the fire, and that might be impolite, so I took off my shield, leaned it against the wall and sat on the floor. Mitch did the same, though he kept the cloak with him, bundled in his lap.

Hilde began pouring something out of a clay jug into some cups, but when she saw us sitting on the floor, she stopped what she was doing and ran to the back of the room.

"Sires, forgive me. You should not sit on the floor."

She dragged a crude chair that had been at the head of the table to the fireplace, then got a low stool that had been next to the cabinet. Mitch took the chair; I got the stool.

Hilde, seemingly still in awe of us, finished pouring the drinks. "You must be weary from your journey," she said, bringing us each a wooden mug filled with frothy liquid. I sipped it. It was vile, but I smiled and thanked her. Mitch did the same.

She stood near, looking at us as if she was watching a bear riding a unicycle. It was a little unnerving.

"How else may I serve you, sires?" she asked.

"You can stop calling us 'Sires' for one," Mitch said.

"We're not knights."

"Yeah," I said. "We're nobody important, so you don't have to keep staring at us."

That made her even more nervous.

"Forgive me, sires, I mean …, forgive me," she said, bobbing her head and looking like she was about to cry.

"It's all right, really," Mitch said. "I'm Mitch, and this is my brother, Charlie. I'm sorry we intruded on you, but this is the only house we know of. It is where Pendragon lived, right?"

"Pendragon, yes, he did live here, many years past."

"When?" I asked. "Can you tell us how long ago that was, or what year this is?"

"I'm not …," Hilde said, still a ball of nervous energy. "It was long ago. Aethelwulf, Aelric's father, was the twentieth son of Pendragon, so Aelric is the twenty-first. But I don't … forgive me."

The pot suspended over the glowing coals wasn't boiling, or even steaming, but I pointed to it anyway. "Don't you think you should tend to that?" I asked, hoping that getting her to do something normal would help her feel normal.

She started to beg our forgiveness again, but then she smiled at me and knelt on the floor. "You are wise, and kind," she said, poking at the unidentifiable gruel with a wooden spoon. I wasn't sure what it was, but I hoped she wouldn't offer us any. "The legends have been around for ages, though I was not privileged to hear them until the day I married Aelric. But who could have thought such a tale might be true? Or that the promised return would happen in my lifetime. Wanderers from a mystical kingdom, brave knights from the ancient times—"

"But we're not knights," Mitch said. "I don't think we're who you believe we are."

Hilde wasn't deterred. "But you are. The legend says brothers—summer twins—will come from a faraway kingdom, carrying a cloak. That is you, is it not? You are summer twins."

I looked at Mitch and shrugged. "If that means we're the same age, then, yeah, but we're not—"

"There is much power in that," Hilde said. Then she looked at the cloak. "And in that."

Mitch held the cloak up. "You were told about this?"

"Yes," Hilde said. "It was how I was to know you were the ones. May I touch it?"

Mitch nodded and Hilde started to get up, but he went around the fire pit and held it out to her. Still kneeling, Hilde slowly, almost reverently, put her hand on it. "I never thought," she breathed, "never, that it could be real. I curse my doubt. It was nearly the ruin of us, of the Land."

"It's all right," Mitch said, returning to his chair. "There's no harm done."

Hilde ignored him. "Even though I had been told the legend, if I had not been warned you were coming, I would have let the dogs see you off. I pale to think what that might have—"

"Warned?" I asked.

"Yes," she said. "Two days ago, a man came asking about you. This is what caused me to wonder if the legend—"

Mitch leaned forward. "This man, was he like a priest, or a holy man?"

"Or a druid?" I asked.

Hilde nodded. "Yes, he wore a grey robe, and he

was very old. He came into the house while I was alone with Edric. It was upsetting, not only because it was improper, but the dogs did nothing to protect us. He seemed to have control over them in some strange way, and this frightened me. He was not unkind, but his urgency felt menacing. He questioned me, demanding to know if I had seen you, and accused me of hiding you."

I remembered the druid who had helped us before. "That sounds like Meryn," I said, "but intimidation, that's not his style."

"Did he have a scar," Mitch asked, tracing a question mark on the side of his face, "on his right cheek, and around his eye, like this?"

"No," Hilde said, "but the other man did."

"What other man?"

I must have asked sharply because Hilde shrank away from me. I forced myself to lean back and take a breath.

"I beg your forgiveness, sires," she said, "if I have caused—"

"No, it's all right," Mitch said. "But we'd like to find this man."

Hilde sat straight. "He was old and dressed in a servant's tunic. I was gathering wood as he passed, and he asked if I had seen two strangers. That was all. I thought nothing of it until the other man arrived later that day."

"And this first man, the servant," I said, keeping my voice calm, "he had a scar?"

Hilde nodded.

I looked at Mitch. "That doesn't make sense."

"It makes sense if that really was Meryn looking for us, but who was the other druid?"

28

I shrugged and looked at Hilde. "And then what happened?"

"Nothing," Hilde said. "They both left, and I have not seen them again. Aelric has been away—"

A sound from the other room made her look up. "I beg your leave, but Edric needs me," she said, rising. She went to what I considered the new room, but it was clear the extension was decades, perhaps centuries, old. From my viewpoint, it looked to be nearly the size of the original house, with a bed, cradle, and a few pieces of furniture in it. There was no door, just a crude archway, and light came in through two small windows, making it a brighter, more cheerful space. As Hilde bent over the cradle, I turned away to look at Mitch.

"What do you think's going on?"

"I don't know. Meryn must have come looking for us, but I don't know who the other guy was."

"Do you think it's significant that they arrived two days ago?"

Mitch shrugged. "It might be because we didn't use the cloak for two days. If we had used it the day we got it, we might have arrived then, but does time run the same way here as back home?"

I didn't get the chance to answer. Hilde returned, holding a knitted blanket bundled against her chest.

"This is Edric Pendragon," she said, bending down and showing us a baby wrapped in the blanket. "Named after my husband's ancestor."

We made appropriate noises. Hilde returned to where she had been kneeling and sat, cross-legged, on the floor, holding Edric to her chest.

"So, your husband is not here?" Mitch asked.

"No, he is here. Aelric returned nearly a fortnight ago, with the rest of the Sussex fyrd. When those men came, however, he was in the fields."

I shook my head. "Fyrd?"

"Yes," Hilde said, "the Fyrd."

She said it slow and loud, like I was thick.

"Pretend we don't know what that means."

"It's the levy," Hilde said, "local men—farmers, shop keepers, craftsmen. The Thegns are obliged to King Harold, and they must provide them to his army."

"Conscripts," I said.

Mitch nodded. Hilde looked confused.

"The levy," Hilde continued, "Aelric was sent with them to join Harold's army on the south coast to stop an invasion by the Bastard of Normandy. They stayed many weeks while their farms lay neglected. But William the Bastard's fleet never arrived, and the levy men were released. Since returning, Aelric has been working long hours—as have the others—to make up for lost days. Now there are rumours of a new attack in the north and fears the levy may be called up again. Then those men came, and I recalled the legend, and I pray this is what you have come to save us from."

To my amazement, while she was talking, Hilde slipped her smock down over her shoulder and held Edric to her exposed breast. I tried my best not to stare or look shocked.

Mitch, who I noticed was also straining to keep his eyes up, asked, "What does Aelric think?"

Hilde looked down at Edric, who seemed to be drifting off to sleep. I hoped that meant she would put her clothes back on soon. "Aelric knows nothing about it," she said.

"Aelric knows his dogs are outside, instead of guarding his home," a voice said.

We all looked to the doorway as a young man with

fair hair and a creased brow stepped through. He was slender, muscular, and tanned, dressed in a knee-length tunic and baggy pants, all made from the same brownish-grey cloth, though it was hard to tell if the colour of the fabric was natural or from grime. He wore muddy boots and held what looked like a garden hoe. And he did not look happy.

"He knows his wife is entertaining strangers," the man continued, stepping forward and brandishing his hoe, "and he knows they are drinking his beer, but he does not know who these strangers are."

Chapter 5

Mitch

"Aelric!" Hilde ran to him, still cradling the nursing Edric to her chest. "What is the news? Why are you home? Are they calling the levy again?"

Aelric pushed her aside. "Who are these men?"

I stood, trying to drape the cloak over my arm to make it look more like a cloak and less like a bundle of cloth. "We are the ones you were told about."

"The knights," Charlie said, standing next to me, "from the olden days."

"You speak nonsense," Aelric said, coming closer. We began to back away, veering to where we had left our shields.

"The legend," Charlie said.

Aelric raised the hoe. "More lies. Are you trying to confound me as you have my wife? Are you scoundrels, or simple beggars?"

I looked at Hilde, still holding Edric. Her face was white. "Why doesn't he believe us?"

"He doesn't know," Hilde said.

Then I began to panic. "You never told him?" I asked, my voice rising.

"My mother-in-law told me," Hilde said, her lips trembling. "And I will tell my daughters. That's how it is passed down."

"So, he doesn't know?" Charlie said.

"What are you talking about?" Aelric asked, turning to Hilde. "Speak sense, woman."

I took advantage of his distraction by dropping the cloak and picking up my shield. Charlie did the same.

"We are friends of Pendragon," I said. "We fought the black knight with him. And now we have returned to help you."

The furrows on Aelric's brow deepened. "Now you speak the impossible. Pendragon lived many generations past."

"He did," I said, "and we were with him, in this very house, he and his mother, Aisley, and father, Garberend."

"They speak true," Hilde said. "They have knowledge I did not reveal."

Aelric shook his head. "A simple trick. You know my lineage. Then who is Pendragon's son, and his son after him?"

"Pendragon wasn't married when we knew him," Charlie said. "He was twelve."

"But I have proof," I said, hoping I was right. I pointed toward the back of the room, where the table and benches stood. "We ate with Garberend, Aisley and Pendragon. And during the meal, I carved a figure into that table. There is no other way I could know about it. Ask your wife. We have only been as far as your fire."

"They have not," Hilde said. "I swear."

Aelric lowered the hoe. "There is a figure," he said, "carved into the table. Tell me what it represents."

I couldn't tell him it was an airplane. That would only convince him we truly were crazy. "It's a cross," I said, recalling how Garberend had straightened out the curves.

The creases in Aelric's brown began to soften. Then he said, "That could be trickery as well. You could have entered our home when all were out."

"But we didn't," I said. "Tell him, Hilde. Tell him what you know."

Aelric looked at his wife. "What have you to say?"

And she told him, about the legend, about how it had been passed down through the ages, about us being knights from the ancient times (which I wish she had left out), about the strange men who had come looking for us, and as she talked she began to cry and the baby started crying too, so Aelric finally laid his hoe down and took Edric, and Hilde put her blouse back on and explained about the cloak—at which time I helpfully held it up for him to see—and by the time she was done Aelric no longer looked angry, he looked dumbfounded, and for the first time, made note of our shields and the way we were dressed.

"You came, dressed like that, carrying those shields?" he asked, after a long and awkward pause.

I nodded. "Of course."

"And you were seen." This wasn't a question.

"Yes. Not by many, but several people did see us as we made our way here."

To my surprise, Aelric smiled. "Then there may be nothing to this rumour, after all."

Hilde, who had come to his side, took Edric from him. "What rumour?"

"I was sent home with the others because a report had reached us. Huscarls, on horseback, are sweeping the land, recalling the levy."

Hilde put a hand to her cheek. "Oh, Aelric, no, they can't. They mustn't."

Then she started to cry again and Aelric hugged her,

being careful not to squash the baby. "There's nothing to fear. Don't you see? It's these men who started the rumour. They are strangely dressed, carrying shields. Of course people thought they were here to recall the levy."

"But they have no horses."

"You know how rumours grow. I'm surprised the gossips didn't conjure up an entire army."

"It still could be true," Hilde said between sobs.

Aelric patted her back. "Hush. All is well. William cannot attack now, he has missed his chance."

"But the north—"

"More rumours. Now put Edric in his cradle. You must help me put everyone's minds at rest so we can get back to work."

It surprised me that Aelric had called us men instead of boys, or children. Then I realized that we were as tall as he was. And it's not that we were tall. I was five-foot-three and Charlie was just a little taller, which made us normal height back home, but Aelric and Hilde, who both seemed to be in their early twenties, were no taller than we were. That turned out to be a good thing because Aelric's plan involved dressing us in appropriate clothing, and the only clothes available where his.

They didn't have a closet stuffed full of things they never wore, like Mom and Dad, there was only a small chest with a few worn tunics and mud-stained pants. Hilde sorted through the sparse collection, selecting a set for me and Charlie. We dressed in the new addition, while Edric slumbered in his cradle. When we finished, we gave our clothes to Hilde, who accepted them as if they were religious relics. Then they had to decide what to do about our shoes.

Again, there was no closet floor heaped with Nikes, just the shoes they wore, and a single extra pair. In the end, Charlie took them. They didn't fit well, and they weren't as rugged as what Aelric was wearing, but they looked less out of place than his sneakers. That meant there was nothing for me to wear, so Hilde gave me her shoes. I was hesitant to take them, but she insisted.

"I go barefoot much of the time," she assured me, even though I suspected it was a lie, "and I will not be without them for long."

She might have been as tall as me, but she had small feet. I squeezed them on and told her they were as comfortable as my own shoes.

"We will go to the village," Aelric told us. "People will be gathering there to discuss the rumours. When those who spied you see you again, they will verify that you are the source of the disquiet and will understand there is nothing to these stories. You will pretend you are recently released soldiers, wandering the countryside, looking for work. There are many such men about these days. That will account for your shields and your traveling cloak."

He seemed pleased with his plan, excitedly making up details, pacing around the fire as he instructed us on what to say and do, and I realized it was relief making him so energetic: he had been more worried than he had let on to Hilde.

"Once the rumours are quelled," he said, "we will go to the fields. When evening comes, we will return and fish the depths of this mystery."

I noticed he had said, "we" were going to the fields. Hilde noticed too. She looked at Aelric, shocked. "But they are guests."

"No," Aelric said, still pacing, "they are former

soldiers looking for work."

And you need all the help you can get, I thought.

This didn't convince Hilde, who obviously held us in higher regard. I hoped she wouldn't leave it at that; I wasn't looking forward to doing farm labour in tight shoes.

"They may have other duties," she said, looking at the floor.

Aelric stopped pacing. "What duties."

"They are knights," she said. "They didn't come to help with the harvest. They came to fight."

"There is no more fighting," Aelric said. "William the Bastard is marooned on the shores of Normandy, and if the Vikings attack, the armies of the North will defeat them."

Hilde lifted her head. "Still, what if these rumours are true? What if they are calling up the Fyrd?"

"They are not," Aelric said. "We have just been released."

Hilde looked at me, her lower lip trembling. "Then why are they here?"

The creases returned to Aelric's forehead as he turned our way. "That is a worthy question." He kept staring at us, clearly expecting an answer.

"I don't know," I said. "We go when we are called. We are at the mercy of the Fates as much as you."

Aelric nodded. "Then let us go see what the Fates have in store for us."

Charlie and I slung our shields on our backs and I bundled the cloak to make it easier to carry.

When we were ready to go, Hilde went to Aelric. "It is a long stretch from two young men with a cloak and shields to armed soldiers on horseback," she said. "Be cautious."

Aelric gave her a quick hug. "There is nothing to be concerned about. We will return within the hour."

But Hilde's face remained a mixture of sorrow and concern.

We followed Aelric out of the house into the warmth of the rising sun. I looked to the sky, which was clear a blue. The sun, though still low, was already warm. Then Aelric stopped and I pulled my gaze back to earth. At the entrance of the farmyard were four armed men on horseback, and about a dozen dispirited-looking men on foot.

Chapter 6

Charlie

I saw the soldiers as soon as we stepped out of the door. Mitch, as usual, was looking elsewhere, thinking deep thoughts, and nearly ran into Aelric, who stood still—and white—as a statue when he saw them.

I knew they were soldiers because they were armed with swords, axes, and shields, wore heavy shirts covered in chain mail, and had helmets on their heads that covered their noses and looked like pointed domes. In contrast, the ragged line of men behind them wore simple clothing, had no armour, and carried scythes and pitchforks instead of proper weapons.

The man on the lead horse dismounted and came toward us. He was stocky, with broad shoulders and beefy arms. He stopped in front of Aelric, removed his helmet and tucked it under his arm. His short hair was plastered to his head with sweat, and his dark eyes, full moustache, and stubbled chin gave him an overall look of menace. "I seek Aelric, son of Aethelwulf."

"I am he," Aelric said, his voice strained. "Who is asking?"

"Reinhart," the man said. "Huscarl of King Harold. The Fyrd is recalled. You must come with us."

"I have done my duty," Aelric said. "I was with Harold's army, waiting for the invasion. William's army never came. We were released, and now the harvest needs tending to."

"A new threat has come from the north," Reinhart said. "Every man must do his duty. And time is short; bring your weapon if you have one, but do not tarry to pack provisions; we will gather them on the way. Now come!"

A scream came from within the house and Hilde rushed into the yard. "No!" She threw herself on Aelric, wrapping her arms around him. "You cannot take him. He has served. We have a child. The harvest—"

"He comes with us," Reinhart said.

Hilde slid to the ground, sobbing, her arms clutching Aelric's knees.

"Fetch your arms," Reinhart said, "and leave the crying woman behind."

Aelric stood still, staring at Reinhart, then he gently pried himself from Hilde's grip and helped her stand. "Be strong," he said, "for Edric's sake. I returned before; I will return again."

Hilde shook her head. "You won't. Not to this world. I feel it." She looked at me and Mitch. "I felt it the moment they arrived; this world, the land, our farm, it's all coming to an end."

Aelric hugged her. "That's your fear talking," he said. "There is nothing to be afraid of." But as he spoke, he glanced our way.

"Come now!" Reinhart bellowed, "Freely or in chains." He turned to the mounted soldiers. "Gerwald, tie him and drag him."

One of the other soldiers—the one with a huge axe strapped to the side of his horse—began to dismount. Aelric stepped away from Hilde and faced Reinhart. "Tell your man to stay where he is. I come willingly. I am now a soldier."

Reinhart laughed. "You are a levy man; you and this rabble will never be soldiers." Then he thrust his face forward, inches from Aelric. "The only use you are to the king is as a shield to protect a better man. Stand, and send your woman to fetch your weapon. I don't trust you out of my sight; you may run like the dog you are."

Hilde, still sobbing, returned to the house. Reinhart watched her go, a humourless smile on his lips, then he turned to me and Mitch, as if seeing us for the first time. "Who are you? With whom do you serve?"

"Their names are Sir—" Aelric began.

"I'm Mitch," Mitch said, "and he's Charlie. "We serve with no one. We are travellers."

"Mercenaries," Reinhart said. "You don't look fit enough to fight your own shadow. To whom is your allegiance?"

I shrugged and looked at Mitch.

"Um, we …," Mitch said. "I guess it would be the President of the United—"

"They are loyal to King Harold," Aelric said.

Reinhart's hand shot out and grabbed Aelric by the throat, pulling him forward until their noses touched. "You speak when I tell you to." He pushed Aelric away, sending him sprawling on the dirt. The soldiers on horseback laughed.

"Enough," Reinhart shouted. "Time is short. We move now." He put his helmet on and strode back toward his horse. "All of you follow behind or we will hunt you down."

"But … we're not soldiers," I said.

Reinhart turned to me and stepped close, breathing sour breath into my face. I struggled to keep my expression neutral. "Then why are you carrying this?" He snatched the shield from my back and examined it. "Such craftsmanship. A waste on someone like you." He threw the shield back. I caught it, but it nearly knocked me over. Then he looked at Mitch. "What is it you have?"

"It's our cloak, sir," Mitch said.

Reinhart grabbed it. "This, too, is a fine piece of work, wasted on you, and no use to a foot soldier." With a flourish, he flung the cloak around his shoulders and fastened the collar around his neck. "This belongs to a man of higher status than you."

"But it's ours," I said. "You can't—"

The next thing I knew, Reinhart's hand was gripping my throat and I was staring into his eyes with my nose pressed up against the metal faceguard of his helmet. "What is it with you lot, who think they can give orders?" Reinhart said. "The next one who tries will be killed on the spot." He pushed me away and looked from me to Mitch. "I don't know who you think you are or what you think you were, but from here on you are levy men serving King Harold, and you belong to me, your body, your soul, your possessions, and your very life. You will do well to remember that."

He turned away, mounted his horse, and led the soldiers—as well as the silent levy men—from the yard without a backward glance. One of the soldiers, the one called Gerwald, turned to the rag-tag band, fingering the blade of his battle axe. It was a fearsome looking weapon, with a single, broad blade and long handle, the type favoured by cartoon executioners. "I look forward to cutting your heads off with this," he said. "So please don't follow us."

Hilde came out of the house, cradling Edric in one

42

arm and an axe—though a much smaller one—in the other. Sobbing quietly, she handed Aelric the axe and held up his son for him to kiss.

"Are you really going?" she asked.

Aelric gave her a quick, but firm, hug. "Huscarl Reinhart speaks true. We must go." He put a hand on Edric's head. "Take care of our son," he said, "and do not lose hope."

Hilde nodded, then looked at me and Mitch. "I will keep your possessions safe. For your return."

We ran from the farmyard, following the levy men until we caught up with the soldiers.

Gerwald looked over his shoulder at us and, with a humourless grin, gripped the long handle of his axe. "Some other time then, eh?"

Chapter 7

Mitch

We followed the soldiers to another farmhouse, then into the village and on to another settlement, adding more men as we travelled. The routine was always the same, and mostly like the scene at Aelric and Hilde's house: men would be summoned, women and children would cry, Reinhart would strut about and threaten and then we would be off, running behind the horses until we reached the next farm.

We tried to keep close to the horses so we could keep an eye on our cloak, but we mostly found ourselves at the rear of the pack, struggling to keep up. Aelric, who wasn't nearly as tired as we were, stayed with us, mostly, though at times he would run ahead and join the main group, casting worrying looks our way. When I could see Reinhart, I noticed he sat tall in his saddle, letting our cloak flutter around him, and when he strutted around, intimidating the latest conscript, he did so with an increased sense of superiority.

"He thinks your cloak makes him a Lord," Aelric said. "He is vain enough to believe theft can give a man dignity."

Soon, we arrived at another small farm, and while we waited for the stunned farmer to extract himself from his wife and children and join our merry band, we sat in the shade, stealing what few moments of rest we could get away with. I was sweating buckets, my lungs burned, my feet were in agony, and I was sure I wouldn't be able to take another step. Every cell in my body begged me to tell Aelric and Charlie to leave me behind. But Aelric wasn't tired, and Charlie seemed to be holding up better than I was (maybe because he had shoes that actually fit) and that made me see beyond the pain. If Charlie could do it, so could I.

When the company moved on, I struggled to get up, and when I did, my feet felt like they were on fire. I noted with shameful satisfaction, that Charlie limped a little and was trying to look as if he wasn't in pain. I took a few tentative steps, then began to trot, but not nearly fast enough. I wanted to catch up with Reinhart, but my legs felt like jelly and the only thing that kept me upright was the knowledge that, if I stumbled, I would never be able to get up again.

Five minutes later, I didn't care what the others thought. "I can't do this," I said to Aelric as I stumbled along, struggling to keep the others in sight. Each word came out as a separate gasp. Aelric, running beside me, was barely breathing hard.

"You must," Aelric said. "If you fall behind, Reinhart will say you are deserting. He will kill you."

Surprisingly, Charlie joined the conversation. "But we'll die of exhaustion if we keep running," he said. "We're not used to running this far."

I wondered what Aelric would make of that. If he really believed Hilde's story, then he would think we were somehow special, and a display of weakness might convince him we really were, as he had put it, scoundrels, pretending to be something we weren't, which we kinda were. But instead of scowling in disapproval, he looked embarrassed. "Of course," he said. "How foolish of me to forget. You would have horses to carry you; soldiers march, knights ride."

"But we're not—" Charlie began.

"Yes," I said. "That's why we can't keep up; we're used to riding."

I expected Aelric to ask why we didn't have our horses with us, and I was scrambling for a way to explain it, but he merely shook his head and said, "Then you must prepare yourselves for some difficult days."

When the sun was high, we rested outside another village. All of us—including the soldiers and the other conscripts—drank from a nearby stream, but while they drank and went back into the village, Charlie and I removed our shoes and soaked our blistered, bleeding feet in the cool water. My shoulder was rubbed raw by the shield strap and every muscle in my body ached. Sitting with my feet in the stream and the sun on my face felt like heaven, but I knew the longer I sat, the harder it would be to get up.

Putting the shoes on was agony, and standing up was worse. I did give a thought to Hilde, who would now be without shoes, but at that moment, I envied her. With Aelric leading the way, we limped across the field and returned to the village to find the others. There were now nearly thirty men, some with shields, some with axes, and some with chain mail, but none with all three. All of us sat in whatever shade we could find, clustered in small groups on the edge of a dusty lot that passed for a town square. We leaned up against a low stone wall, away from the others. Aelric stayed with us, though he kept looking at the nearby groups as if he would rather join them, even though they kept glancing our way with suspicious, and occasionally hostile, looks.

"Why do the men keep looking at us like we've done something wrong?" Charlie asked.

"You are strange to them," Aelric said, rubbing the back of his neck, "and they fear what they do not understand. Also, you worry them."

I tried to stand but slipped back down against the wall. Fortunately, my shield protected my back, but the clanking caught the attention of the other men, who again cast unfriendly looks our way. Aelric took my arm and helped me up. Charlie managed to stand without Aelric's help, though he did need to lean on his shield. Once upright, he slung the shield over his shoulder, wincing at the pain. "Why do we worry them?" he asked.

Aelric shuffled his feet and looked at the ground. "They fear you are slowing the company down. I have heard the others talking. We are to meet Harold's army in London tomorrow at noon, so we can march to York with them. If we fail to reach them in time, they will leave without us."

As if on cue, Reinhart shouted for us to fall in. Beyond the clusters of men, the soldiers—Gerwald and the two others—mounted their horses. Then I saw Reinhart, sitting tall in his saddle, still wearing our cloak. He turned his horse and the four of them trotted away, followed reluctantly by the levy men, and even more reluctantly, by us.

I took a tentative step and nearly fell. Charlie limped behind me. "How far is London?" he asked.

Aelric, already in the lead, turned and looked at us, his expression a mixture of resignation and apology. "From here, nearly thirty miles."

47

◆

In the afternoon, we started north, leaving the villages, farms and rolling field behind as we made our way toward London. With the larger company, Reinhart was forced to slow the pace a little and, though still in agony, Charlie and I were better able to keep up. We were also on a proper road, broad and flat with drainage ditches on either side. The road surface wasn't in the best condition, but it was better than the farm tracks we had been trudging through all morning, so the going was easier and more orderly.

Occasionally we met other people—travellers heading south, a farmer with a cart, peasants carrying loads on their backs—but Reinhart and his soldiers never slowed. They kept to the road, forcing anyone in their way into the ditch. In this way, we covered a great distance. But as the sun began to set, Reinhart's soldiers began riding among the men, shouting, kicking, cursing, trying to make them move faster because the company was not as near to London as he had hoped. Despite their efforts, as the light dimmed the men slowed, and when darkness drew in, we stopped.

By then, I was in such a fog of pain, I barely noticed. I had simply been moving forward, one agonizing step at a time, and when Reinhart led the company into a nearby field, Charlie and I stumbled over the uneven ground and fell onto the grass the moment Reinhart called a halt.

"We camp here," Reinhart said, riding his horse among us and looking down with undisguised contempt. "We move again before dawn. Double-time."

With great effort, I sat up, my body aching and my stomach rumbling. I looked at Aelric, who seemed tired but not in pain, and felt a momentary pang of jealousy, which I quickly suppressed; none of this was his fault. "We're just going to sleep here in this field?" I asked. "With no food or water or blankets?"

Aelric shook his head. "There is water nearby, and this field has been well-chosen; it has grass and brush for making beds and fires."

"But we're hungry," Charlie said. "We've been walking for hours without food. Even Reinhart can't expect us to go without something to eat. Or is he planning to starve us to death?"

Aelric rose to his feet and stretched, groaning a little as he did. "Build a fire," he said, "I'll get water. Then we can make beds. Food will come."

Aelric and most of the levy left, presumably to get water, leaving me, Charlie, and a handful of others behind to start fires. Reinhart, still wearing our cloak, strutted about, shouting abuse at the men for their failure to make better time. Meanwhile, his soldiers— Gerwald, along with the other two, Hoban and Blekwulf—erected their camp with practiced efficiency. Almost before Aelric was out of sight, a tent appeared, and one of them was starting a fire.

With supreme effort, I sat up.

"What do you think Aelric is going to say when he comes back and finds out we haven't done anything?"

Charlie continued to lay on his back, his shield at his side. "I don't know, but I can't start a fire. Can you?"

I looked at other groups of men who were gathering bedding and starting their own fires.

"We can at least start pulling up grass to make

49

something to sleep on."

Charlie didn't move. "Knock yourself out."

It was clear he wasn't going to help, but I couldn't let Aelric come back without us having done something. Before I could get to my feet, however, Reinhart walked by.

"You two," he bellowed. "More trouble than you're worth. If you keep us from making London on time, I'll hand you over to Gerwald. See if you can walk faster without your heads."

Then he turned away, our cloak fluttering around him in the evening breeze.

Charlie sighed and sat up. "Easy for him to say; he gets to ride a horse."

Slowly, painfully, I pulled up as much of the long grass as I could. Charlie helped, and by the time Aelric returned, carrying a leather bag filled with water, we'd amassed a small pile. He tried to not look disappointed, but I could tell he wasn't really pleased with our lack of progress.

Aelric had drank his fill at the stream. At least I hoped he had, because Charlie and I finished off the water while he gathered wood and made a fire. Once it was lit, we flopped down on the matted grass, and I fell instantly asleep. The next thing I knew, Aelric was shaking me awake. I sat up, dazed and disoriented. It was full dark, and cold. Above us, an impossible number of stars glowed in the black sky.

Aelric nudged Charlie, who opened one eye. "Leave me be," he said. "I was dreaming of food. I could smell it."

"It is food," Aelric said, "come to the fire."

Trying to stifle my groans, I limped to the low fire, where Aelric was already sitting cross-legged on the ground. When we both settled next to him, he pulled a stick from the fire. On the end of it was a seared hunk of meat. He broke it into chunks with his bare hands and the three of us wolfed it down, along with some bread and cheese.

"Where did all this come from?" I asked between mouthfuls.

"There is a village nearby," Aelric said. "The supplies came from there."

Hungry as I was, I hesitated. "I don't suppose this was given willingly."

Aelric drank from the refilled water bag. "It is a privilege to support their King. I am sure they gave with joy in their hearts."

"Yeah," Charlie said through a mouthful of cheese. "Joy at not having their heads cut off."

We ate, drank more water, and then wrapped ourselves in some thin blankets Aelric gave us. I was sure they had been liberated from the same village the meat had come from, but I was too tired to worry about it.

I started to take my shoes off, but Aelric stopped me.

"I know it feels bad," he said, "but if you take your shoes off, your feet will swell, and you will not be able to put them on in the morning. Do you want to walk the rest of the way to London in bare feet?"

The thought terrified me. I left my shoes on, and so did Charlie.

"Sleep now," Aelric said. "Tomorrow will be harder. We are behind schedule. Reinhart will rouse us early for a quick march to London."

"How much further?" I asked.

Aelric shrugged. "Fifteen miles, maybe less. If we

rise before dawn, and march at a quick pace, we could surely join up with Harold's army before noon."

I grimaced at the thought. Charlie, sitting next to me, leaned close. "I can't walk fifteen yards on these," he said, pointing to his feet, "let alone fifteen miles. Especially if that's just the warm-up for the real thing."

"You must," Aelric said, "or you will die."

With that cheery thought in mind, I pulled my stolen blanket around me, laid down on the grass and fell asleep.

Chapter 8

Charlie

"Get up, we leave soon."

I opened an eye. It was still dark. I tried to move but every part of my body felt like it was on fire. The skin on my face was tight and hot, my shoulders burned, my leg muscles knotted, and my feet were simply lost in a fog of agony. I raised myself slowly from my grass bed, peering into the grey morning. The stars were fading, the grass and my blanket were wet with dew, and I was shivering from the cold. I smelled smoke, however, and cooked meat, and the stench from the area the company had designated as a latrine, which was suspiciously close to where we had camped. Next to me, Mitch groaned and slowly sat up. From the look on his face, it was clear he felt no better than I did.

"You'll feel better once you move about," Aelric said. "Eat now. Then fold your blankets so you can carry them."

A few small fires glowed in the dim light. Beyond, hidden by the gloom, men shuffled and groaned and packed. I pulled the blanket tight around me, trying, but failing, to ward off the chill. Aelric shared what little food we had left. He had not started a fire, so it was nothing but a small lump of cold meat and a hunk of stale bread. Still, I couldn't have been more grateful if he had offered hot pancakes and bacon smothered in syrup. I stuffed it into my mouth and washed it down with the few gulps of remaining water. No one had given any orders yet, but the feeling in the camp was one of urgency, so I forced myself to stand.

Mitch struggled with his blanket, awkwardly folding and knotting it as Aelric had shown him. "Help me with this." he said.

While Mitch groaned, I stuffed the blanket under his shield to try to keep the pressure off his back. When I finished, he said exactly what I had been thinking: "This isn't going to work, and I'm not going to make it out of this field, with or without a pack."

Carefully, I put my shield on, easing the strap onto my sore shoulders. I didn't bother having Mitch try to cushion it, I just carried the blanket in my arms. When I tried to take a step, my feet felt like I was treading on hot spikes.

Mitch, limping beside me, shook his head. "This doesn't feel right. We've had hard times before, but nothing like this."

"Maybe this isn't where we are supposed to be," I said. "You know, it's still dark, and the camp is in chaos, so no one would miss us if we—"

A hand grabbed me roughly and spun me around. The pain was instant and stunning. My instinct was to attack but I found myself face to face with Aelric and my balled fist stopped in mid-swing.

"Do not say such things," Aelric hissed. He glanced furtively around. "Do not even think it."

"We're just talking," I said. "It's not like we've made a decision."

Aelric, his hand still clutching my shoulder, shook me. "It is not to be considered. Do you understand?"

Before I could answer, or give him a punch in the

mouth, a disruption from the far end of the camp caught our attention. Although we couldn't see anything, we heard Reinhart bellowing and feet running in several directions. Other voices rang out. There was more shouting and arguing. Then calm returned.

"What was that?" Mitch asked.

"I know not," Aelric said. "I expected orders to move on, but none have come."

"So, what do we do?"

"We wait."

Gratefully, we returned to our mats. We weren't expecting anything more than a short nap, but when Aelric shook me awake, it was full daylight. For a few moments, as my stiff muscles protested and my many pains reawakened, I regretted the extra rest, but as I limped along at the rear of the company, I felt as if I might be able to keep walking. For a while, at least.

The nightmare of the previous afternoon returned—the road, the soldiers, my careful concentration on putting one foot in front of the other—but after a while, I noticed something different.

"Step lively you dogs," came a shout from behind. "I'll not have you costing us any more time."

I glanced over my shoulder. "How come Blekwulf is walking behind us?"

"And where's Reinhart?" Mitch asked.

"Gone," Aelric said.

It might have been good news but, thinking of our cloak, I blanched. "For good?"

"No. He's gone to fetch Edward."

"Who?"

"Edward, of the south wood. His dwelling is near mine. I know him. He deserted."

We walked in silence for a time, with Aelric strangely subdued.

"Was that the disturbance we heard this morning?" I asked. "Was Reinhart angry when he found out?"

Aelric answered, his head down, staring at the road in front of him. "Yes, Reinhart was very angry. He went after Edward, to bring him back. Gerwald and the others were to wait a time and then move on if he did not return."

"Did he come back?"

Aelric shook his head. "Not yet. And we are now too late to join Harold."

"But Reinhart has our cloak," Mitch said. "When will he be back?"

"Do not fear for your cloak," Aelric said without looking up. "Reinhart will return. And when he does, he will have Edward with him. Fear for Edward, not your cloak."

Although we were on the Roman road, we did not keep up the same pace as the previous day, a small advantage that I was hugely grateful for. According to Aelric, when Edward had slipped away, he had taken one of the horses, so Blekwulf, Hoban and Gerwald took turns walking at the rear of the company to keep an eye on the remaining levy men, and the soldiers did not like walking any more than the levy men did. Reinhart had planned to reach London by noon, but with the confusion caused by the deserter, and the soldiers taking turns walking, it was lunchtime before we got our first glimpse of the city.

I saw it while we ate our meagre meal, sitting atop a small rise. In the distance, a low cloud—grey and dingy, like a smudge on the horizon—floated over the flat plain. Aelric told us it was London, or, more precisely, the smoke that hovered over the city. It didn't appear all that far away (it was close enough, in fact, that when the breeze was right, it brought with it a whiff the city's stench) but on foot it would take two or three hours to get there, and Harold's army, if they were on schedule, where already marching north.

These facts did not sit well with Gerwald, Blekwulf and Hoban because, while we ate, they patrolled the perimeter of the group, stone-faced and wary. And when our short rest came to an end, they held a brief council some distance away, well out of earshot. Gerwald and Blekwulf sat on the two remaining horses, talking down to Hoban. When they finished their conversation, they ordered the company to move out. As before, the horses, carrying Gerwald and Blekwulf, rode ahead while Hoban brought up the rear. What changed was, we left the road and turned onto dirt tracks that wound and crisscrossed through the countryside.

"They are taking us around London rather than through it," Aelric explained, when I asked what they were thinking.

"But that would have been faster, and easier," Mitch said. "And we could have got more supplies."

"And half of our number would have disappeared into the lanes," Aelric said. "Finding a single deserter on a stolen horse in open country will not be difficult for Reinhart, but if we all scatter like rats, Gerwald and his two men will be hard pressed to capture any of us, and they would have to report to Reinhart that they lost us."

I glanced over my shoulder at Hoban to be certain he was out of hearing range. "But even here," I said between gasps. "It might be worth a try. There are only three of them. If we all ran—"

"I would speak no more if I were you," Aelric said sharply. "Conserve your strength. You will need it."

We marched in silence for a time, more slowly and often in single file due to the narrow lanes. Then Aelric said. "I apologize if I offended, but when you see what happens to Edward, you will understand my concern."

"Do you think Reinhart will catch him?" I asked.

Aelric nodded. "From what the others have told me of Reinhart, his cruelty is matched only by his resourcefulness. He will keep his promise; he and Edward will be with us by morning."

"Less talk," Hoban shouted from behind. "And you two, march like men. Soldiers in Harold's army do not walk like women."

General laughter erupted from the company that Hoban could do nothing to quiet. I felt myself go red and saw that Mitch was trying to stand straighter and walk without limping. Fighting against the pain that each footstep brought, I squared my shoulders and tried to march.

We rested and marched and rested and marched some more. Because of the confusion that morning, there was little food and no water, only what we could find during our rest stops. We marched on paths and rutted roads. We marched through villages and past farmsteads. We marched over flatlands and hills, through forests and marsh. At one point, we forded a river, and I left the waist-deep water shivering, and marched on in sodden pants and shoes, my muscles cramping and my skin burning as the world spun before my eyes.

Our pace slowed; the miles crawled by in inches. After a time, I fell into a trance, moving one foot in front of the other, ignoring pain, thirst, hunger, the hot sun, and the hard earth beneath my feet. By the time the sun was nearing the horizon and the air was beginning to cool, we had left the smoking, smelly city behind and were on another remnant of a Roman road running north.

As dusk began to settle, we left the road and set up camp outside a small village. Once again, the soldiers commandeered meat, bread and blankets, and this time, to my shame, I felt nothing but relief when I received my share of the stolen food.

We ate, warmed ourselves by the fire, then laid down with our blankets. Tired as I was, I slept fitfully, feeling too cold, too hot and, in the early hours, plagued by pain I could actually hear pounding in my head. Thud. Thud. Thud. But when I woke up fully, I realized it was the sound of horse hooves. I raised myself up on one elbow and peered into the darkness. Outlined by starlight, I saw two horses trotting through the camp. There was a rider on the lead horse, but the one following carried only a large bundle. Next to me, Aelric sat up to look.

"Who is that?" I asked.

"Reinhart," he said.

"Where's Edward?"

Aelric laid back down and stared into the night sky. "That was him, on the second horse, tied to the saddle."

I shivered, even though I still felt hot. "How did Reinhart find him? How did he find us?"

"I told you," Aelric whispered. "You cannot escape Reinhart."

"Now what," I asked.

Aelric turned over and pulled his blanket around

him. "You will find out soon enough. Sleep now; morning arrives soon."

Chapter 9

Mitch

We were awakened before dawn. I sat up, shivering, my blanket wrapped around me, my head woozy. Mist covered the camp and, one by one, fires came to life, flickering in the gloom like giant fireflies. Aelric lit our fire and we sat around it, warming ourselves while we ate a cold breakfast and waited for the call to move on.

My feet throbbed with pain, pulsing in hot crescendos with every beat of my heart. I was cold, but sweating, as if we had already marched ten miles in the hot sun.

We were, as always, separated from the main group, which was clustered together some distance away. If it wasn't for us, Aelric would be with them, and I felt equally grateful and guilty that he chose to stay with us. Being with the others wouldn't solve our problems, but it would be warmer, and safer. From the main camp, the smell of seared meat and a murmur of voices drifted our way, while we sat in silence.

Dawn came, the fog lifted, and Aelric built up the fire. And we waited. Soon, the sun threatened to peek above the horizon, and still, we did not move.

When the sun appeared, the activity in the camp increased, but still no one gave the order to march.

"What's going on?" I asked. "Are we getting a day off?"

Aelric gave a bitter laughed. "There is no such thing. We will march, and it will be at a quicker pace to make up for the late start, as soon as the ceremony is over."

I looked at the camp, now gathering into a tight group, clearly expecting something to happen. Aelric started toward it, beckoning for us to follow but giving no explanation.

Simply standing was an effort, and each step brought fresh pain, but I limped along with Charlie and Aelric until we got to the rear of the cluster where we were still unable to see what was going on. Then Reinhart's voice cut through the silence. "Spread out, the lot of you. Everyone is to witness this."

The men shuffled into a large semi-circle around Reinhart, Gerwald, Hoban and Blekwulf. In front of them knelt the deserter, Edward, bound hand and foot, his face puffed and bruised, his tunic stained red. Reinhart, dressed in gleaming chain mail, with our cloak hanging from his shoulders, stepped forward. He drew his sword and pointed it at the kneeling man.

"This man, this worm, thought to return to his farm and family while he was bound by oath to Harold and sworn to protect this land. The conditions of his oath are well-known to this coward, as they are to all of you." Reinhart pointed his sword at the levy men, moving it in a slow arc until we all got a good look at it. "And you all know the punishment."

Satisfied, he rammed the sword back into its scabbard and nodded to Gerwald. The prisoner's sobs grew louder as Gerwald stepped toward him, and when Gerwald raised his fearsome axe, Edward began to scream.

The blood drained from my face. "He's not going to …"

"Yes," Aelric said.

I turned my head. "I can't watch."

Aelric grabbed me by the shoulder. "Do not look away. Reinhart is watching. He will punish those who flinch."

I turned back, but closed my eyes, praying Reinhart wasn't looking my way. I heard a dull thud, then the morning fell suddenly silent. When I opened my eyes, Edward's body was slumped on its side. Blood pumped onto the wet grass, making a red slash that ended where the man's head lay, staring into the sky.

Reinhart, now mounted on his horse, rode in front of us. "That fate awaits all who break their oath," he said. "Now move out."

"I think I'm going to be sick," Charlie said.

I nodded. "Me too."

"Do not falter," Aelric said. "It will be seen as weakness or, worse still, sympathy for the condemned man. In Reinhart's current mood, that may be enough to see you next in line for Gerwald's axe."

"But they killed that man," Charlie sputtered, "just for running away."

Aelric grabbed his arm and pulled him close, glancing nervously around as he hissed in his ear. "Keep your voice still. You must not let others think you believe the punishment unjust."

"But it was," I said, keeping my voice low. "All he did was run away; surely he didn't deserve that."

Aelric released Charlie. "The world you come from must be strange indeed," he said, looking at the ground and shaking his head. "If men who forsake their sworn oath are not made an example of, then every man in the fyrd would disappear overnight. How do your kings fight without an army? Would you have Harold

63

face his enemies unaided?"

"No," I said, "but I would rather he faced them without us."

Aelric sighed. "I thought you were brave knights. Get your shields, we move out promptly."

We set off at a brisk pace, with Blekwulf and Gerwald riding beside us, barking orders, forcing us to march in formation.

"You will be marching like soldiers by the time we join with Harold, or you will be dead in a ditch."

With memories of the deserter, and his punishment, so fresh in my mind, I tried my best to step sharp and in unison. Charlie and I brought up the rear of the double-wide column, with our shields and makeshift packs on our backs, struggling to keep up. My breath burned in my throat and the world seemed to tilt and waver. Strangely, my feet didn't hurt any more, but that was because I couldn't feel them.

As the sun rose higher, a bank of clouds covered the sky and light rain began to fall. It cooled the air and wet my clothes, but I still felt hot. Hour after hour I kept moving, one foot forward, then the other, then the other, feeling as if I was walking under water. At some point, I became vaguely aware that the company had stopped. I heard voices, some raised in greeting while others shouted commands. Scruffy farmers with tools for weapons joined our group of levy men, and all around were burley men with short hair and moustaches, wearing military tunics and carrying shields. There were carts and horses and an old man with long, grey hair sitting on what looked like an over-sized wooden wheelbarrow filled with cooking pots. The old man watched me as I shuffled slowly by and it occurred to me that, even though the company had stopped, I was still walking. Charlie was with me, his eyes glazed, stepping forward, in time with me, like a sleepwalker, or a zombie.

Ahead, talking with more soldiers, stood Reinhart. He glanced our way. I saw his mouth move but his words became garbled. He laughed, and then the world tilted, and the road rose up, slamming me in the face.

◆

"I expected as much." Reinhart's voice. "Seen it plenty of times, men marching until they drop from exhaustion." Pain as a boot nudged me. "Are they dead?"

A hand, cool and soothing. "No."

"They will be soon enough. Leave them. We've wasted enough time already."

"If we leave them behind, they will die."

"A happy outcome; they have been nothing but a burden."

"We could take them in the carts."

"It was bad enough that they were a burden to me, I'll not have them burden my horses." The voice receded, moving away.

"I will take them on my barrow."

A pause.

"You will not leave one pot behind because of them." Reinhart, louder, closer. "And if you fail to match pace, I'll have the heads of all three of you."

"Yes, sir."

Then silence, and darkness.

Chapter 10

Charlie

For a long time, I dreamed. I dreamed I was lying on a stone-strewn beach that rocked to the rhythm of the waves. Hot sun burned me, cold winds chilled me, and ocean waves soothed me. I dreamed of our cloak, and of blood, and men without heads. I dreamed of marching, of Saxons, of the broad, wooded expanses bordering the Roman roads, but never of home, for even in my dreams I knew that, unless we retrieved our cloak, this was my world.

At times I rocked, at times I floated. Darkness came and went. Water wet my parched lips and cooled my dry throat. Gentle hands rubbed my wounds and, slowly, the fires that burned my feet, my shoulder, my head, eased. My dreams became less troubled, my breathing less laboured and, many hours and many miles later, I opened my eyes.

I blinked. My eyes felt dry and crusted. Beside me, Mitch stirred.

"What's that smell?" he asked, pushing aside the thin blanket that had been covering us.

I tried sitting up, but the world spun. "Dizzy," I said, slumping back onto the straw mat. Then I looked at Mitch and started to laugh.

He scowled. "What's so funny?"

"You." I pointed at his face, which was covered in

green slime. "You look like the booger-man."

"So do you."

I put a hand to my cheek. "What the …"

I propped myself on my elbows, waiting for the spinning in my head to subside, trying to get my bearings. We were in a small tent, lit only by a slit of dim light filtering through the flaps. As my eyes adjusted, I saw that our feet were bare and covered in the same green paste as our faces. The smell coming from the paste was bitter and it permeated the tent. Outside voices shouted orders, carts creaked, metal clanked, and horse hooves clopped.

Slowly, I eased myself into a sitting position. "What do you think's happening?"

"I don't know," Mitch said. "The last thing I remember was meeting some soldiers. Do you think we should investigate?"

I looked at his face. "Probably, but I don't want to chance running into Reinhart looking like this."

Then the tent flap opened, making us jump. But it wasn't Reinhart, it was an old man wearing a short tunic, pants made of something that looked like burlap, and a leather cap pulled low across his forehead. His hair was long, merging into his flowing beard and moustache so that all you could see of his face was a pair of eyes and a nose poking out from a tangle of grey. He stooped low to enter the tent, bringing with him the smell of wood smoke and two bowls of stew.

"I thought I heard voices," the old man said. "Sorry if I startled you, but I thought you might like something to eat."

He knelt on the ground and set the bowls down next to us, making me suddenly realized how hungry I was. Still, the strangeness of the situation made me hesitate.

"Go on," the man said, "eat. You must be famished."

The stew was hot and tasty and thick with vegetables and meat. We scooped it up with wooden spoons, stuffing it into our mouths. I felt self-conscious with the old man sitting there, watching us eat, but I was too hungry to care. It wasn't until I had scraped the last of it out of the bowl that I finally turned to look at him.

"Who are you?" I asked.

The old man stroked his beard. "I am Malcolm."

I looked at his tunic and beard. "You're not a soldier."

Malcolm shook his head. "No, I am a cook. I belong to Reinhart."

"His slave?" Mitch asked.

This made him laugh. "Sometimes he treats me as such, but I am merely in his service. He keeps me with him because he finds me useful. And he likes my rabbit stew."

"I recognize you," I said. "You were on the road. I remember seeing you just before ... whatever happened. What did happen?"

"Exhaustion got the better of you. You were, quite literally, on your last legs."

"You saved us," I said.

Mitch nodded. "That's right. Reinhart wanted to leave us lying in the road. We'd be dead if it wasn't for you."

"I put you on my barrow," Malcolm said. "Hardly a heroic deed. It was far more heroic of you to hold on as long as you did. You kept going until your company caught up with us. If you had fallen earlier, you surely would have been left behind."

The agony of the forced marches came back to me, and I suddenly feared what lay ahead. Then I flexed my arms and legs. They were stiff, but not sore. "How long have we been out?"

"You slept through the night, then for a day and a night," Malcolm said. "And a day and a night, and another day. Night is coming upon us now."

"Three days!" A flurry of questions spun in my head. "What happened? Where are we? Why is this stuff all over us? Who—"

Malcolm held up a hand. "Slow down Charlie. I can only answer one question at a time."

"You know our names?"

"Certainly. Your friend Aelric, he is most worried about you. He told me your story."

"So where are we?" I asked.

"You have travelled far in your sleep; we are now a few miles west of Lincoln. York is less than two days journey from here."

Mitch sighed. "So, we're still marching."

"Your travels are far from over," Malcolm said. "And now that you are awake, you won't be getting any more rides on my barrow."

I shook my head in disgust and slumped down on the mat. "Can't you put us back to sleep?"

"I could," Malcolm said, "but I believe you will find yourselves fit enough to walk now."

"I do feel better," I said. "Come on, Mitch, try standing up."

Slowly, I stood, stooping slightly in the small tent. Mitch stood next to me. We stretched and flexed our legs.

"This is amazing," Mitch said. "I feel better than I

did before we came here. Is this green stuff some sort of miracle cure?"

Malcolm shook his head. "No, simply healing herbs."

I rubbed some paste from my forehead and sniffed my finger. It smelled bitter, with a strong scent of garlic, though that might have been the stew. "Is it like those new herbal medicines we see in the vitamin store at the mall?"

"This is ancient medicine," Malcolm said, "from days when men and the land lived in closer harmony. Most have forgotten the healing power of the land. There are few of us who remember."

I touched my shoulder where the shield strap had rubbed it raw; the wound was closed now, the skin taut and firm. For the first time, I wondered where it was, and where our clothes had gone. Both me and Mitch were in bare feet and wearing loose tunics that came to our knees and reminded me of hospital gowns.

I looked down at Malcolm, who was still kneeling. "Where are our shields?"

"And our clothes," Mitch added. "And what's Reinhart going to do to us?"

Malcolm smiled. "You must be well if you are concerned about returning to your duty and facing your punishment."

Feeling better was one thing, going back to Reinhart and the forced marches another. "I'd rather not return to either of them."

"I shouldn't worry too much," Malcolm said, gathering up the empty bowls. "Reinhart isn't likely to execute you for being unconscious. But if he finds you have awakened and did not report to him, he would be right to be angry. You'd best find him before he finds you."

I sighed and rolled my eyes. "Can't you tell him we died and sneak us out of the camp?"

Malcolm laughed. "Do not lose heart," he said, rising and standing, as we were, stooped in the low tent. He looked at us, suddenly serious. "Many trials await. This is not the road we were intended to walk, but our journey must start from where we are. And the sooner, the better." He turned to leave. "There is a bucket of water behind the tent. Wash yourselves. I will fetch your shields and new clothing, better suited to what lies ahead."

"Wait," I said. "What did you mean by 'our' journey?"

"And what trials?" Mitch asked.

Malcolm turned to face us. "All in good time."

Then I saw his eyes—piercing and blue—and the scar on the side of his face that ran up his cheek and disappeared beneath his cap.

"You're the druid," I said.

Mitch nodded. "You're Meryn."

Malcolm's expression never wavered, giving no indication if we were right or wrong. But neither did he appear surprised. "I have many names," he said. "Here, I am Malcolm."

Chapter 11

Mitch

"It must have been Meryn," I whispered.

"How could that be," Charlie said, keeping his voice low, "no one could live that long. We were with Pendragon when we met him; that must have been hundreds of years ago."

"But he was also there when we were with the Romans, and that was long before we met Pendragon."

"How long?"

"How should I know? All I know is that we're here, and so is he."

I listened for Charlie's response but heard only the sounds of the night—the chirping of crickets, the hoots of faraway birds and an occasional rustling in the dry grass we hoped was a fox or raccoon and not a bear. Then, after a few minutes of silence, he said, "I suppose. But do you think that means we're here for the same reason? Does everything we're going through have something to do with that rock, the whatchacallit."

"The Talisman," I said, shrugging even though he couldn't see me. "We won't know that until we can talk with Meryn, or Malcolm, again."

The sound of movement made me snap my mouth shut and stare straight ahead, into the darkness.

We were standing guard duty on the outskirts of the

72

camp. Behind us, the soldiers had bedded down for the night. Next to them, the levy men slept in their own camp. And next to their camp was a smouldering fire and three mats of dried grass. Aelric was sleeping on one of them, and we would be sleeping on the other two as soon as we were through being sentries.

Having avoided the hardships of the previous days, it seemed churlish to think of standing in a field holding a shield and a spear as punishment, but it wasn't as easy as it sounds. And if Malcolm hadn't done such a good job of making us well, and providing us with better clothing, we wouldn't have been able to endure it.

It was enough of a relief just to have shoes that fit, but they were also sturdy and comfortable, and Malcolm had given us something resembling socks, which helped cushion my feet. Our new pants and shirts were made from light, but durable material, and we each had a small cloak to help ward off the evening chill. I was as comfortable as I had been since arriving nearly a week ago, which was a good thing, because Reinhart was trying to make up for the suffering we had missed (as if nearly dying from exhaustion was something we had done on purpose merely to give ourselves an excuse to malinger) by making us stand out in a field all night.

Thankfully, because he had been preoccupied with planning the march and calculating how and when we would catch up with Harold's army, we'd had only a brief meeting with Reinhart, where he had barked and insulted and ordered us on double guard duty and dismissed us, adding that he expected to see us on foot for the remainder of the march. At first, we felt we had got off lightly, but then we had talked with Aelric.

73

"This is serious," Aelric said. We'd found him at an isolated campfire, looking tired and worn. "He means you ill."

"But all we have to do is stand there," I said. "We're capable of that."

"It's tedious standing in the dark looking at nothing."

"Is he hoping we'll die of boredom?" Charlie asked.

Aelric sighed. "He's hoping you'll fall asleep."

"Will that get us in trouble?"

Aelric shook his head and looked at us in disbelief. "The punishment for falling asleep on guard duty is death."

"Oh."

So now, hours later, we stood—holding our shields in one hand and borrowed spears in the other—struggling to stay awake. Reinhart had ordered us to stand far from the camp, ostensibly to provide adequate warning if an enemy appeared, but it was also far enough away where we couldn't hear anything and had nothing to see but stars. In such isolation, succumbing to sleep was more of a danger and, despite my renewed energy, I soon felt fatigued.

But now, as the stealthy sound behind us drew nearer, I was having no trouble staying awake.

"What do we do?" Charlie whispered.

"I don't know. Shouldn't we at least turn around to see what it is?"

A twig snapped. We whirled around. Charlie brandished his spear. "Halt, who goes there? Stand and be recognized!"

From out of the gloom, with our cloak draped around him, Reinhart appeared. "So, still awake. I'm disappointed."

"I thought you'd be pleased, sir," I said.

"Pleased?" Reinhart barked. "I was practically on top of you before you heard me. You might as well have been asleep."

"We weren't expecting an attack from the direction of the camp, sir," Charlie said.

Reinhart stood close to Charlie, glaring directly into his face. "Always expect the unexpected."

I feared Charlie might be cuffed or kicked, but Reinhart turned away and strode back toward camp. "Another hour for your insolence."

We turned to face the empty field, standing straight, holding our shields and spears. Reinhart would not have been pleased to know it, but his visit had jolted me awake and, for now at least, my eyelids weren't as heavy.

"We've got to find a way to talk to Malcolm," I said, when I was certain Reinhart was far enough away.

"When?" Charlie asked. "You just know we're going to be here all night. Then we'll be marching, then Malcolm will be busy feeding Reinhart's men, and then we'll be back on guard duty."

I sighed. "Yeah. But we need to get to him somehow."

Charlie grunted. "Before we can do that, we have to figure out a way to not fall asleep."

"True," I said, scanning the night sky, my thoughts turning to Reinhart, Malcolm, our cloak, and the Talisman, "and to continue to expect the unexpected."

Chapter 12

Charlie

We were awakened at dawn after a scant few hours' sleep. The morning was bright but cold, and I shivered under my thin blankets. No fires were lit. We ate cold cheese and bread, packed our few provisions, and prepared to march.

In the soldier's camp, the activity was orderly and brusque. The men dismantled the tents, packed the carts, and began marching from the field toward the Roman road, forcing the levy men to scurry to catch up. It was a larger company now. The soldiers we had met on the road—Reinhart's full regiment—numbered about forty men. The ragtag band of levy men, which had numbered thirty or so last I knew, now totalled almost fifty. We marched in a long column, two abreast, flanked by soldiers on horseback and a number of carts. At the rear of the soldier's column, Malcolm pushed his barrow, piled high with metal pots and cooking apparatus as well as his own tent and blankets. Seeing him, I marvelled that he had found the room for us, or that he had the strength to push the barrow, especially with us on it.

Behind Malcolm were the levy men, separated from the soldiers as they marched, just as they were separated when they camped.

"How come the soldiers and the levy men don't

mix," Mitch asked Aelric, who was marching in front of us. As usual, we were in the rear, even though we felt fit enough to walk at the front of the column. "I thought we were all in the same army."

"The soldiers are the army," Aelric said. "That is their profession. We are farmers who know nothing of war. They are our betters."

I looked at the columns stretching ahead of us. The soldiers stepped sharp, each carrying a weapon. Their chain mail and shields were being transported for them, but they still wore heavy military tunics and metal helmets. Despite this, they kept up a steady, even pace.

The levy men, dressed in whatever clothes they were wearing when Reinhart took them, were less orderly and, like Aelric, walked with a stooped and weary gait. They didn't march, they tramped. Few of them carried weapons, fewer had shields.

"But, if we camped and marched together, it would benefit both groups," Mitch continued, even though it was clear that Aelric wasn't in the mood for conversation. "The soldiers could teach the levy men and the levy men could help the soldiers with their work."

"Again, you speak of your strange customs as if you can impose them here," Aelric said, an icy edge to his voice. "The soldiers are not our comrades. Do not speak to them, follow their orders, and keep out of their way. That may keep you from getting killed before we get to the battle. Now close your mouths and move your feet. Those of us who have not had three days of rest are too tried to march and talk; we can only do one or the other. And it is marching that keeps us alive."

I looked at Mitch, who shrugged. We walked on in

silence, Aelric's sharp word ringing in my ears. Aelric's friendship, as tenuous as it was, was the only thing keeping us from being totally isolated from the company. The idea of losing it was unsettling. But I had to admit, he—and the rest of the levy men—had a right to be angry.

We were rested, having lain sleeping for three days in the cart just ahead of them. We were unfit for any task—farm or soldier-related—and yet we had warrior shields. And we were strangers. All of this conspired to keep us separate from the levy men. And Aelric, due to nothing more than our untimely arrival and subsequent proximity, was considered one of us.

As the sun rose, the cool morning turned into an unseasonably warm day, hampering the pace of the levy men, and forcing the soldiers—who had to be sweating under their heavy clothing—to slow down. In addition to that, the Roman road in this part of the country—wherever that was—was narrow and neglected, making progress difficult. Still, Reinhart drove us on, marching us up hills and down hills, through thick forest and open farmland.

When we crested one of the larger hills, I saw a rolling vista of wheat-coloured meadows and trees shimmering red and gold in the sun. It reminded me of autumn back home and at once made me feel buoyant and sick with longing. The company—soldiers and levy men alike—ignored the view.

By noon the sun was relentless, and, after a quick lunch, the heat caused the company to move noticeably slower. Reinhart, Gerwald, Hoban and Blekwulf rode among the soldiers and levy men, shouting, cajoling, threatening, but the pace continued to flag. Eventually, the more fatigued levy men were allowed to ride on the carts for short distances, which made me feel mildly vindicated. The soldiers were not offered the option of riding, not that they would have accepted it; they would march until they dropped rather than admit to weakness.

During the afternoon, our stops became more frequent, though they were kept short, and dinner—cold meat and bread—lasted no longer than any of the short rests. We gobbled our food while sitting in the road and were ordered back on our feet as soon as we swallowed our last bite.

As sundown approached, we did not stop to make camp. The weary levy men fell further behind and me and Mitch, in order to keep up our pace, found ourselves at the head of the levy column, not far behind Malcolm and his barrow. Despite our growing fatigue, we quickened our pace to catch up with him. Reinhart would not be pleased with us infiltrating his unit, but Malcolm's was the only friendly face in the entire company, so we put Reinhart out of our minds and fell into step with Malcolm.

The old man was surprisingly fit, but long days of pushing the barrow, and the march over the uneven road and rough terrain, was taking its toll. Instead of feeling comforted by being in the company of someone who looked favourably on us, I felt a deepening shame, knowing that we were the ones who had sapped his strength.

"Can we help at all," Mitch asked.

Malcolm smiled at him. "The barrow is heavy; I doubt you could push it very far." He plodded on, sweat streaking down his brow. His hair, his beard and his clothes were all damp with sweat.

"Surely there is something we can do to help," I

said.

"There is only room for one to push. It must be me."

"Why are we still walking?" Mitch asked after a few minutes of silence. "We should have stopped an hour ago."

"Reinhart believes we are not far behind Harold's army. He desires to join up with them by nightfall."

"But, what if we don't?"

The barrow came to a lurching stop as one wheel hit a rock. Malcolm stumbled forward but regained his balance. I kicked the rock away and threw my weight against the wheel to get it moving again.

Malcolm, panting slightly, nodded his thanks.

I looked at Mitch. "We can't help push," I said, "but we could pull."

As Malcolm plodded forward, we got ropes from the barrow, tied them to the front and looped the ends around our chests. Straining against the ropes, we pulled as hard as we could, and the barrow began to move faster.

We were now far enough in front of the levy men, and far enough behind the soldiers, that no one would be able to hear us if we talked, so I asked the question that had been burning inside me ever since I had first seen Malcolm.

"Was it you who came looking for us at Aelric's?"

I had to turn my head and call to him to be certain he had heard, then I turned back and continued pulling. For a few minutes, I heard nothing, and I assumed he wasn't going to answer. Then he said, "Yes, I was expecting you. I found Aelric's wife outside her home and exchanged a few words with her, enough to know she had no knowledge of you."

We were supposed to have been there by then, weren't we," Mitch said.

"That is true," Malcolm said, after another pause, "and it was troubling that I could not find you. My aim was to return, but Huscarl Reinhart was ordered to recall the levy, and I had no choice but to go with him. We can thank the gods, or the Talisman, that we were united, but the delay puts us in an awkward position."

"You mean, because now we can't get away from Reinhart?" I asked.

"That is part of it—it is true we cannot leave without endangering ourselves—but there are other considerations."

He said nothing more. I wanted to know what the other considerations were, but instead I asked, "Who was the other man?"

Malcolm's reply came immediately. "Other?"

"Hilde told us that, on the same day you visited, another man—someone dressed like you usually are, with a robe and all—came and asked about us. She said he was rude to her, and a little frightening."

Malcolm said nothing for a long time. I was going to ask him if he had heard me when he finally said, as if to himself, "This is disturbing, indeed. And it changes all."

We were catching up with the soldiers by then, so I didn't ask any more questions, and Malcolm didn't provide any further explanation, which didn't surprise me in the least.

Soon after that, the sun disappeared and the welcome chill of the evening drew in, but still we marched. Twilight came, and then full darkness. Without the benefit of light, we stumbled on the uneven pavement and tripped over stones. Marching became impossible, even for the soldiers, and the column moved forward by inches. Then Reinhart rode into view.

"Cart horses, now, are you?" he roared. We froze, certain he wouldn't miss the opportunity to hand out more punishment, but he merely shook his head in disgust. "At least you have made yourselves useful." Then he turned to Malcolm. "Stand down. We camp here for the night."

Malcolm set the barrow down. "Shall I prepare a proper meal for the men?"

"They, nor you, will have time for such luxuries. Sleep here, next to the road. We will rise early and, God willing, join the fight."

"Yes, sir," Malcolm said.

"Secure your barrow and report to my camp," Reinhart said as he rode away. "You will make me rabbit stew before I retire."

"Help me get this off the road," Malcolm said. Then he stepped close to me and Mitch and spoke in a quiet voice. "There is much to discuss, but now is not the time. I must report to Reinhart, and you must stay with my barrow."

We pulled and pushed as he selected a few pots from the cart.

"It is important you remain here," he said, as we settled the barrow and blocked the wheels so it wouldn't roll down the slope. "Do not return to the levy, and do not mix with the soldiers."

I nodded and he turned to go. Then he stopped.

"And find your friend, Aelric. Bring him here. The three of you will camp around my barrow, to guard it."

"But what if he doesn't want to come?" I asked as he walked away.

"Tell him he must," Malcolm said, as he continued up the road, "if he wishes to see another sunset."

Chapter 13

Mitch

"Wake up! You will see battle this day."

I opened my eyes. The sun had not yet risen, and the land was shrouded in thin, grey mist. All around, up and down the road, men saddled horses, loaded carts, grabbed weapons, and snatched a bite to eat.

"Help me pack the barrow," Malcolm called. "We are moving out now."

Aelric, who had agreed to join us (after some cajoling and half-truths about obtaining a more favourable position within the army), was already up and helping Malcolm. Charlie was just dragging himself from his mat but managed to rouse himself enough to help us get the barrow loaded and manoeuvre it onto the road. The soldiers ahead of us were already moving out, stepping quickly, not marching.

"Double time!" came Reinhart's voice from the head of the column.

Charlie, Aelric and I ran ahead to help pull the barrow, but Malcolm called us back. "That is not necessary. We have not far to go"

We fell into step with him, moving at a slow jog as the barrow clattered over the cobbles

"What's going on?" Aelric asked.

"The enemy has been sighted. There will be battle soon."

Charlie looked at Malcolm. "You're kidding. How did ... where ...?"

"Reinhart sent scouts ahead last night," Malcolm said. "They caught up with Harold's army. They are at Tadcaster, a few miles away."

"Are they fighting the Vikings now?"

Malcolm shook his head. "Not yet. Harold has sent scouts to York to assess the situation. They will have returned with news by the time we reach them. Whatever their news, there will be battle this day." He sighed. "Many who watch the sun rise this morning will not see it go down this evening."

I felt a chill run through me. "Are we going to be in the battle?"

"Perhaps."

"But," Charlie sputtered, "we don't know how to fight."

Aelric, still holding his axe, smiled, "War is simple."

Malcolm shook his head. "You have much to learn. But stick close to me, and you will be safe."

We jogged for what seemed like hours, with the mounted soldiers exhorting and threatening the men whenever they began to flag. Dawn came slowly, with grey clouds covering the sky, but soon a cool breeze blew, and the day cleared just as the sun rose over the horizon.

Soon after, we crested a hill and, as the soldiers in front reached the summit, they began to cheer. This spurred the rest of the company on. Aelric, Charlie and I took up the ropes fastened to the front of the barrow. We pulled and heaved while Malcolm pushed and, together, we moved the unwieldy barrow up the rise. As we reached the top, we saw why the soldiers were cheering.

In the distance, glowing in the morning sun, lay a walled city. Outside the city, covering a broad, flat plain bordered by a narrow river, was a sea of people, stretching as far as I could see. Everywhere I looked there were soldiers and levy men, tents, smoking fires, horses and wagons. And all through the throng, weapons and chainmail glinted in the sun. We stopped where we were, mesmerized by the spectacle. Then the barrow rolled forward, and we grabbed the sides to keep it from careening downhill.

"That's a lot of people," Charlie said.

Aelric nodded. "Yeah, there's not an enemy in the world who could defeat such an army."

Malcolm, pulling back hard on the barrow's handle to keep it from rolling away, shook his head. "You have much to learn of warfare."

Soon, the road levelled out, and with our objective in sight, the company picked up pace and we had to jog to keep from being pushed from behind. The trailing levy men cheered as they spotted the army from the top of the hill while, up ahead, the lead soldiers were already clasping hands with Harold's men.

"The Vikings can't have more people than this," Charlie said. "Can they?"

"Size is not always the deciding factor," Malcolm said. "The quality of the soldiers, the intelligence of the leaders, their strategy, the will to win, all these matter as much, or more, than size. You would do well to remember that."

Malcolm looked over the army spread out before us as if assessing them.

"Look at the many men in the field," he said. "What do you see?"

"Well, soldiers," Charlie said. "Lots of them."

"And levy men," Aelric added.

"Yes," Malcolm said. "Harold has many men, but a large portion of his army is made up of farmers with rakes, scythes, and hoes for weapons. Men who have no armour and who have never seen battle. The Vikings did not invade with farmers. The enemy are all battle-hardened soldiers. And do not forget, Harold's men—soldiers and levy men alike—have been marching hard for days; the Vikings are well rested."

Charlie began looking a little uneasy. "But we have more men, right?"

"There are nearly ten-thousand men on this field," Malcolm said. "Reports of the Vikings say they number nearly thirteen thousand."

We continued in silence for a while, both Charlie and I staring at our feet as we moved closer, one step at a time, toward what I was sure was certain doom.

"We don't stand much of a chance," I said. "Do we?"

Malcolm chuckled. "Do you not listen? True, they are greater in number, but Harold is a cunning warrior. And our soldiers, tired as they may be, have the will to win."

"So, you think we'll win?" Charlie asked.

"We have a good chance," Malcolm said, "for Harold possesses another great advantage that the Vikings know nothing of."

The question was left hanging. After a minute or two, Aelric filled the silence. "What advantage?"

"He's talking about the Talisman," I said.

"I am," Malcolm said. "As long as the Talisman is safe, no invading army can conquer the Land."

"So where is it?" Charlie asked, "And how do we know it's safe?"

"That is why you are here: to guard the Talisman."

"I thought we were here to fight the Vikings."

Malcolm shook his head. "This is not your battle; if you fight today, you will die. For now, you must leave the fighting to others."

"But Reinhart is never going to allow that," I said.

We turned the barrow off the road and entered the field, heading to where Reinhart's company was setting up camp.

"Leave that to me," Malcolm said.

Chapter 14

Charlie

We made camp on the edge of the field, Reinhart and his soldiers near the bulk of the army, and the levy just outside the main group, where the rest of the levy men were gathered. By the time we rolled the barrow into position between the two groups, the soldiers were already lounging on the grass under the growing heat of the morning sun. Reinhart rode among them, glaring down from his horse, with our cloak still draped around him. He looked grim but said nothing, then he rode toward the centre of the encampment, followed by Hoban, Blekwulf and Gerwald.

Me and Mitch, and even Aelric, flopped down, ready to fall asleep, but Malcolm began unloading the barrow.

"There is enough firewood in the barrow to get you started," he said. "You'll need to gather more, but first get a fire going, fill the big pot and boil some water."

I lifted my head but didn't get up. "What? You want us to cook? Now?"

Malcolm continued as if I hadn't spoken. "When one fire is built and the pot is heating, build another." He pulled several bags from within the barrow and dumped them on the ground. A few beets, onions, and turnips—along with some other unidentifiable vegetables—tumbled out. "Cut these up, put them in the boiling water, save some for the second pot." He held up another, smaller bag. "Put a handful of these herbs in each pot."

Mitch sat up and blinked. "Why—"

"In war, you take every advantage. Every one. We have the advantage of a short rest; make use of it."

I had thought I was making the best use of it, but I didn't think Malcolm would agree, so instead I said, "But the soldiers will think we're crazy, cooking dinner when we're supposed to be preparing for war."

"They will think what they want of you, but they will go to battle rested and fed." Malcolm dropped the bag of herbs on top of the vegetables. "Hurry now, there is no time to waste. You don't know how long you have."

Mitch stood, stretched, and yawned. "What are you going to do?"

"There are matters I must attend to," he said. "And I have a few rabbits to catch."

Then we found ourselves alone among the vegetables.

"Your friend is strange," Aelric said, "but he speaks true."

"What do we do now?" I asked.

Aelric began arranging wood for the fire. "You heard him. Take those pots and fill them with water. I will start the fires."

By the time we returned with the water, Aelric was working on a third fire. We helped him put the wrought iron frames around them and hung our two pots from the liveliest of the two.

"Cover those pots," Aelric said. "Charlie, help me with the vegetables. Mitch, get more water."

I supposed I could have felt resentful at his ordering

us around like that, but to tell the truth, I was glad to be told what to do. And it was something I wasn't unfamiliar with. Mitch, too, seemed happy with Aelric taking charge, and, without a word, headed off with another large pot toward the distance stream.

Aelric found a collapsible table among the jumble of unfamiliar items in Malcolm's barrow. It was small and had a scarred top, but it made chopping the vegetables a lot easier, and I was glad Aelric had thought to look for it because it never occurred to me and, if it had, I wouldn't have recognized it for what it was.

"Cut the vegetables into smaller chunks," he said, checking the two pots and building up the fires beneath them. "The water is not yet boiling, and little pieces will cook faster."

"It would save a lot of time if we just put them in a microwave and zapped them for a few minutes."

Aelric shook his head. "What are you saying?"

I picked up another potato. "Nothing."

Mitch returned and took over chopping while Aelric sent me for wood. I scrounged around for as much as I could carry, which wasn't easy because the area was pretty well picked over. By the time I returned to our little camp, the vegetables were boiling in all three pots, and Aelric was adding the herbs.

As the smell from the bubbling pots drifted over the field, men began looking our way. Soon, smoke from other fires rose into the air and the camp became thick with the smell of woodsmoke and boiling vegetables. Half an hour later, the pots all contained a thin, vegetable soup with a pleasant aroma and a bland taste. I worried what the men would think if we portioned it out to them, but then Malcolm returned, carrying a sack, and resting a pole over his shoulder with half a dozen rabbits dangling by their back legs from it. By now, the aroma had drawn a few of the levy men and Malcolm put them to work skinning and chopping.

He added meat to the pots of soup (telling the men to take the excess rabbits to the other camps), put in more herbs, and mixed in some flour to thicken it. Soon, the concoction had turned from a thin soup to a thick and tasty stew, and I understood why Reinhart so valued Malcolm's service.

The soldiers and levy men from our company, and others, lined up, and we spooned the thickened stew into bowls or the men's helmets. It was gone within minutes, but as we began to clean up, we saw lines forming at other campsites and I realized that Malcolm had used us as exampled to the other cooks, who would not want to be outdone. As a result, the whole army had been fed, instead of simply waiting for word to go into battle.

"Harold and his Thegns will be back from York very soon," Malcolm said as me and Mitch cleaned out the big pots and Aelric gathered the bowls. "We will move out shortly."

Around us, soldiers sharpened swords, strung bows, put on chainmail and adjusted their helmets.

"Something has been puzzling me," I said, as I handed Malcolm another pot. "How is it that you are able to catch rabbits so quickly?"

"I don't catch them," Malcolm said, arranging the gear on his barrow. "They come to me."

"Why would they do that?"

"I know their language."

"Really. You expect me to believe—"

I was cut short by a commotion behind us and turned to see Reinhart, Gerwald and several other soldiers on horseback ride into the camp. Despite the rising heat, the soldier on the lead horse wore gleaming chain mail, polished leather boots and gloves. He was thin, with shoulder length black hair parted in the middle, a pencil-line moustache and small, dark eyes. Behind him, among the soldiers, was an old man wearing a dusty robe. He was bare headed and had long white hair and a beard like Malcolm. I turned to ask Malcolm who he was, but Malcolm wasn't there.

The thin man dismounted, and the others followed his lead.

"So, this is the Sussex levy?"

Reinhart nodded. "Yes, Lord Falan."

"And these are your cooks?" Falan stared at me, and I shuffled uncomfortably. I looked away from him to find that the old man was staring at Mitch.

Reinhart looked surprised, as if noticing us—and the empty stew pots—for the first time. "Yes, my Lord."

Falan glanced around at the collection of levy men and soldiers, finishing their meals. "Your cooks seem better prepared than your army. You must keep them safe. They are a valuable asset."

Reinhart scowled at Aelric and me and Mitch. "My men will be ready."

"See to it."

Falan turned back to his horse. As he prepared to mount, the old man in the robe placed a hand on his shoulder and whispered in his ear. Falan nodded, climbed into the saddle, and looked down at Reinhart.

"Your cloak," Falan said. "How did you come by it?"

Reinhart, unable to hide his surprise, looked at me and Mitch, and then up at Falan.

"I won it in fair combat, my Lord," he said. "It is mine by right."

I wondered if we should object, but a sideways glance from Reinhart convinced me to stay silent.

"I am your Lord," Falan said. "And what is yours is mine by right. Give it to me."

My mouth dropped open. I tried to say something, anything, but no sound would come out. Reinhart looked up at Falan in shock. "But my Lord—"

Falan held out his hand and, while Falan's soldiers watched, Reinhart removed the cloak and gave it to Falan. I looked at Mitch, who was, like me, watching the scene in disbelief and horror, as the rest of Falan's troop mounted and trotted away.

Around us, the soldiers and levy men made a point of looking away from Reinhart as he flexed his fists and grew red in the face.

"Your cloak," Aelric said.

Mitch drew a deep breath and let it out slowly. "Yes, our cloak."

I shook my head. "We'll never get it back now."

Reinhart turned to us. "Your cloak?" he said. "It was mine. Now it belongs to Lord Falan. You, however, still belong to me, not as soldiers, or levy men, but as my dogs. Now clean up this camp and pack up the carts. We move out soon"

With that, he mounted his horse and rode toward the centre of the camp. The soldiers and levy men also moved away, leaving us alone in the cluttered campsite. I shook my head, wondering how, and if, we would ever get home.

"I see the thief has, himself, been robbed."

I turned to see Malcolm standing behind us.

"Malcolm," Mitch sputtered. "Did you see? That man … Lord Falan … our cloak. We'll never get out of here now."

"Why does everyone keep taking our cloak?" I asked.

"It is no coincidence," Malcolm said. "The cloak seeks the Talisman. This is what I feared would happen."

"What? What is happening?"

"There will be time for talk later. We must pack now; we are marching to war."

Chapter 15

Mitch

The army moved quickly and soon we were, once again, marching up the road. But, despite us being in the rear helping Malcolm with the barrow, it didn't feel like the dreaded forced marches of the previous days. The levy men, carrying rakes and hoes and scythes, marched with the soldiers, who were fitted with armour and carrying shields and swords and spears. And, despite the hardships of the previous days, they didn't slouch or drag their feet, they marched upright, their heads held high, and seemed eager to move faster. Up and down the line, the army thrummed with energy.

Now that we had joined up with the rest of the army, being in the rear meant there were others with us, soldiers and levy men alike, pushing barrows, driving overloaded carts, or just walking with huge sacks on their backs. We should have been marching with the Sussex levy and Reinhart's soldiers further up the road, but after telling Lord Falan that we were cooks, Reinhart didn't dare put us in the front lines. He didn't exactly order us to stay with Malcolm, he just sorta ignored us, which suited me and Charlie fine, though I suspect Aelric would have rather been marching with the soldiers.

Word had come to us that, after conquering the city

of York, the Vikings had demanded treasure and hostages. The entire Viking army was now waiting in a large plain just east of the city, where they were expecting the delivery of gold and slaves. They were not expecting Harold's army.

As we neared the walls of York, the army split, with the soldiers and most of the levy men heading east to meet the Vikings, leaving two thousand levy men behind to set up camp in a field near the city. Their orders were to hurriedly construct the camp and then join up with the army, which by then would be engaged in battle. Only a handful of soldiers and levy men were selected to remain behind to keep watch over the camp, among those were Malcolm and, by extension, me, Charlie and Aelric.

We were relieved at that, but many of the others were not, especially Aelric.

Malcolm got straight to work, Charlie and I breathed a sigh of relief, and Aelric complained.

"I waited weeks on the south shore for an army that never came," he said, kicking at the dirt, "and now I have marched for days and, instead of fighting, I'm doing common labour."

I didn't point out that he wasn't doing that, either. Around us, the grassy field, nestled in a curve of the River Ouse, was in a frenzy of activity, and soon Malcolm had us digging fire pits and setting up tents, while Aelric followed us around moaning.

"I don't know why you're in such a hurry to get killed," I said after it was clear he wasn't going to help us.

Aelric snorted. "I want to see battle. You're supposed to be brave knights, you're here to help us, why are you content to avoid the fight?"

I shook my head. "That may be, but we're not here to go to war."

"Only cowards shrink from battles," Aelric said. "It is your duty to fight."

Then Charlie turned on him. "And only idiots go looking to get killed."

Our words might have become hotter if Malcolm hadn't stepped in. "You all have much to learn of battles and warfare," he said. "I suggest you join forces and finish setting up this camp. If you work together, you will finish in no time."

"What's the point in hurrying," Aelric said. "We have all day."

"You were ordered to set up camp, you are not a prisoner. Finish as much as you can. I will secure horses and permission to leave."

I felt the blood drain from my face. Aelric beamed. Charlie gulped. "Are you going to take us to the battle?"

"Yes," Malcolm said, "if you work hard. I will return shortly. Have your shields and, Aelric, your axe."

We worked as a team after that, and I wasn't surprised to find that Aelric, when busy instead of bitching, was worth the two of us put together, although that may have been because our enthusiasm had dimmed. Aelric helped us erect tents, fetch water, and dig pits, and soon the camp was more or less ready.

Soon after, Malcolm returned, riding a horse and leading another. In one hand he carried a shield, and a sword hung at his side.

Charlie gaped at him, open mouthed. "Where did you get all this?"

"All this," Malcom said, "is my own. The horses I borrowed." He indicated the riderless horse following him. "Aelric, you ride this one. Mitch, ride with Aelric, Charlie, with me. Hurry, our time is short."

Charlie climbed up behind Malcom while Aelric and I mounted our horse.

"Are you taking us to war?" Aelric asked, a smile on his face and optimism in his voice.

"No," Malcolm said, as he turned his horse and led us from the camp. "To school."

We galloped along the road after the soldiers, and then into the fields, climbing a ridge that provided a view of the countryside. Soon we saw the dust cloud raised by the stamping of thousands of feet, and pushed on faster, catching up and then passing the army as it moved slowly toward the enemy. I gripped Aelric, trying to stay on the back of the horse without the benefit of a saddle, while my shield bounced against my back. Malcolm, with Charlie clinging to him, led us off the rise, and we galloped through the shallow valley for what seemed an eternity. When I thought I couldn't hold on any longer, we went back up the rise, but at a mercifully slower pace.

As we neared the crest of the low hill, Malcolm eased his horse into a slow walk and signalled for Aelric to do the same. "We will have a good view from here," he said. "But we must keep low. Do not be seen."

We tied the horses to a withered tree, left our shields and Aelric's axe, and continued on foot, crouching as we neared the top, and then crawling on our stomachs. Malcolm motioned for us to be silent, and we followed him, moving inches at a time. We crawled to a clump of low bushes, then squirmed beneath them, well camouflaged. When I saw what lay on the opposite side, my breath caught in my throat, and I realized the need for caution.

Not far away (in fact, close enough to smell), on an expansive meadow cut through by a river, were hundreds—no, thousands—of men. They were clustered near the river, occupying both sides, which were linked by a narrow bridge. Some were lying in the grass, eating and drinking, some were fishing, and others were swimming. Most were dressed in light tunics and loose trousers, though many on our side of the river were shirtless and wearing only what looked like a loincloth. They were brawny, broad-shouldered men with long, blond hair, beards, and tanned, weathered faces. They lounged on the grass, their eyes closed, bathing in the hot sun. None had weapons.

"That's the biggest picnic I've ever seen," Charlie whispered.

Malcolm did not smile. "That is no picnic," he said. "That is the Viking army."

I looked closer at the men on the far side of the river. Lying on the ground amongst them were swords, shields, battle axes, and lances, though there was none of the heavy armour I had seen Harold's army wearing when they had marched out of the camp.

"What are they doing?" Aelric asked. "Why aren't they preparing to fight?"

"This, my young friend, is your first lesson," Malcolm said. "In war, you are never safe." Then he looked at me. "What did you see as we rode up here?"

I thought for a moment, then said, "Nothing."

Malcolm nodded, but didn't speak, letting the silence stretch on. Then Aelric's face lit up. "There were no guards. They posted no sentries. They don't believe they are in danger."

"Correct," Malcolm said. "Now look here, on the far side of the river. See the low rise beyond the army, and the men waiting there?" We all nodded. "One of them is Tostig, King Harold's brother. He is often impulsive in his quest for revenge, but the other man, King Harald Hardrada, who commands most of this army, is a skilled warrior and gifted commander. Yet he, too, has forgotten the first rule of warfare. He has allowed himself to be seduced by victory. Having defeated the armies of the north, he now waits here for tributes of gold and hostages, confident that Harold is still in the south. It is his single mistake, but it will cost him dearly."

Some of the soldiers sleeping in the grass closest to us, suddenly lifted their heads. Then a few others turned, gazing down the road that cut through the meadow and crossed the narrow bridge. On the far side some began to pick up their weapons.

"Look there," Malcolm said, "those who have kept their minds clear know something is about to befall them. Their head is trying to convince them that what they hear is the rumble of gold-laden carts, but in their hearts, they know they are doomed."

Now I could hear it too, the tramping of feet, the clopping of hooves, and they were coming quickly. On the far side of the river, more soldiers grabbed for their weapons. The tramping grew louder, and my head felt light as the enormity of what was about to happen sunk in.

"Time for one more lesson before the battle begins" Malcolm said. "What is the best way to assure your survival in a fight—be it a brawl or a battle?"

"Never be taken by surprise," Aelric said, staring at the scene unfolding in front of us.

"Always have the advantage," Charlie said, his face white.

Malcolm shook his head. Then the first of the soldiers arrived, the mounted Huscarls, followed by the armoured soldiers, charging forward, screaming, their lances thrust ahead of them, their axes swinging around their heads. In the meadow, the unarmed Vikings leapt to their feet, but many had hardly enough time to run before they were cut down.

The battle began barely a hundred yards from where we lay hidden, close enough to hear the cries of the wounded, to see the blood flowing over the ground as arms, legs and heads were cut away from fleeing Vikings. Guts spilled onto the ground as swords and axes cut men in two, and the air filled with the stench of shit and piss, and the tangy scent of old pennies.

My blood went cold, my face grew hot, and I felt sure I was going to throw up. In the melee, another unarmed man fell, screaming, to his knees, his left shoulder hanging away from his body, blood spurting, as the soldier behind him pulled back his sword and ran on to his next victim.

I took a deep breath, fighting to keep my meagre breakfast down.

"The best way, the only sure way, to survive a battle," I said, "is to not be in it."

Malcolm nodded. "You have discovered an important truth," he said. "Never forget it."

Chapter 16

Charlie

The slaughter was beyond imagining. The Vikings were packed against the riverbank and Harold's soldiers cut into them like a buzz saw through a side of beef. And with the same result; blood and body parts piled so high the soldiers had trouble climbing over them. Those who slipped on the slick battleground were set upon by the Vikings, killed and stripped of weapons, which were turned on the Saxons. The peaceful meadow ran red with blood, and hundreds of Vikings lay dead or, even worse, dying. The mass of bodies writhed with screaming men, some without limbs and others frantically scooping their intestines back into their bodies. Shouts, the clash of swords, and the whinnying of terrified horses filled the air. I looked at Aelric and was pleased to see that he, too, looked horrified.

"I think I'm going to be sick," I said.

Malcolm backed out from under the bush and stood, gazing down at the battle. "A fitting reaction, for it is a sickening sight." He motioned for us to join him. "The need for stealth has passed. Come now for a better view. The battle has just begun, and many lessons remain."

To my surprise and dismay, Malcolm led us further down the slope, closer to the battlefield, where the sights, sounds and smells became even more terrifying. The armies were clustered around the bridge now, with the Vikings struggling to escape across the narrow span. It had only been a matter of minutes, and already nearly half of them were dead, but the slaughter continued. "Why don't they stop? Hasn't Harold won? I mean, look at that." I pointed at the carnage, my hand shaking.

"It is a good start," Malcolm said. "But take your eyes off the bloodshed. Tell me, what else you see."

Mitch spoke almost at once. "I see a band of Vikings being slaughtered by an army five times their number."

"And across the river," Aelric added, "I see thousands of Viking soldiers getting ready for battle."

I looked and saw he was right. The Viking army was rushing to form a defensive line along the top of a rise, standing close together, holding their shields in front of them.

"Harold enjoys the advantage at the moment," Malcolm said, "but the longer it takes him to move his army across the bridge, the more time his enemy has to prepare. By the time the two armies meet, their numbers will be nearly even, and Harold will have lost the advantage of surprise."

Barely ten minutes had passed and the hundreds of Vikings on our side of the river were already reduced to a small band, fighting madly to keep Harold from crossing the river. Despite having no armour, or perhaps because of it, the Vikings were taking a toll on Harold's men. Wielding the axes and broadswords they had taken from the fallen Saxons, they roared and charged into Harold's soldiers, spinning, slashing, shouting, gouging, and killing a dozen or more before they, themselves, were finally brought down.

Harold's men had chainmail and helmets, but they were little use against a whirling battle-ax, and in the oppressive heat, the weight of the armour sapped their strength.

Across the river, the Vikings continued to strengthen their line. Before them, on horseback, rode the commanders, King Hardrada and Tostig, exhorting the men. Then, from behind the line, three horsemen galloped away. I watched them, wondering, and trying to think like a commander.

"Those men on horseback, where are they going?"

"A worthy question," Malcolm said. "And one Harold is probably asking himself, for he knows there are three thousand Viking warriors guarding their ships ten miles away at Riccal."

"They'll bring reinforcements," Aelric said.

"How long before they get here?" Mitch asked.

Malcolm stroked his beard. He looked remarkably serene despite the horrific scene unfolding in front of him. "The horsemen will take less than an hour to alert the reserves," he said. "Then the men will gather their weapons and set out for the battle as fast as they can."

"So, around three hours," I said. "If Harold hasn't won by then, he will need to have a significant advantage."

Malcolm nodded. "That would be wise; it is best to prepare for the worst, and that means every minute counts."

I looked to the river. The carnage on our side was almost complete. Nearly every Viking was dead and the last of them were falling back across the bridge.

"Harold certainly has the advantage now," Aelric observed.

"In war, nothing is certain," Malcolm said. "Fortunes can change in an instant. See now what is happening."

The Saxon army, at last, controlled the bridge. Harold rode to the front of his army, ready to lead them across. But then a Viking walked onto the bridge—a bare-chested, broad-shouldered giant— carrying a huge, double-bladed battle-ax. The Saxons were startled into silence. The Vikings looked on with admiration.

He shouted something I couldn't make out, which made the Vikings laugh and cheer. Then he held the axe up and swung it over his head, shouting some more as the Vikings cheered louder and the Saxons stood in mute disbelief.

"He is challenging Harold's army to fight him," Malcolm said.

"One guy, against all of them?" Mitch asked.

"The army can only face him one at a time," Malcolm said.

"It's still one against thousands," I said.

Malcolm nodded, "But he doesn't have to win, he merely has to delay them."

Then a soldier stepped onto the bridge and approached the Viking. The Saxon, wielding a broadsword and wearing chain mail, was smaller, but nimbler, than the Viking, and displayed both skill and courage as he advanced. In an instant, the giant cleaved him nearly in half.

The Viking army erupted, cheering, stomping the ground, shouting insults. Another Saxon soldier stepped onto the bridge, more cautiously this time. Within seconds, his body fell next to his comrade.

Me and Mitch and Aelric, as well as the Saxon army,

watched in stunned horror as the Viking killed one soldier after another. Soon, they began attacking in groups of three or four, but by then the bridge was slick with blood and piled high with dead Saxons, giving the giant Viking the advantage. As the men tried to throw the bodies off the bridge or scramble over them to get to the Viking, their bodies were added to the pile.

"He's holding off an entire army," Aelric said. "Single-handedly."

"Every minute counts," I said, recalling Malcolm's words, "and he has already given them ten."

At the front of the Saxon army, I saw Reinhart, riding a horse, shouting orders to his soldiers and the levy men he had with him. Three of them ran onto the bridge. And three more bodies fell.

Aelric gaped at the dead Saxons, those on the bridge and floating in the water, and those littering the meadow, intertwined with the bodies of the Vikings. His face paled. "Those are my comrades," he said. "My countrymen, my friends."

"That is the fruit of war," Malcolm said. "And why it must be avoided, or ended quickly."

But there seemed no end to the mayhem. The Viking, though bleeding from numerous wounds, carried on, the bodies piled higher, and beyond him, the Viking army cheered while continuing to strengthen their defensive position.

"They've got to get over that bridge," Mitch said.

"They've lost nearly forty men already," I said. "They've gotta see this isn't working. They need to try something else."

"What else can they do?" Aelric asked.

As if in answer to his question, a boat appeared on the river, heading for the bridge. I looked closer and saw it wasn't a boat, but a barrel, cut in half, with one of the levy men sitting in it. He was young, hardly more than a boy, wearing no armour and carrying only a slender spear. He waited in the barrel, unnoticed by the Viking, until he was beneath the bridge, then he jumped out and scrambled up the structure to where blood dripped between the slats. There he waited for the giant to meet the next group of Saxons. When the Viking stood above him, he thrust his spear between the slats.

The Viking roared in pain, then slowly sank into a sitting position, his bloody axe lying next to him. The Saxons didn't cheer and stream across the bridge. Instead, they stared, stunned and shaken, until Harold came forward and ordered them to move.

They cleared the bridge, unceremoniously dumping the bodies of their comrades, along with the Viking, into the river. Then the army streamed across, forming up a line to face the Vikings.

"See what they do," Malcolm said. "How they interlock their shields to form a wall."

The Saxons now outnumbered the Vikings, so their shields were close together, tightly locked. Above them, on the rise, the Vikings stretched their line, weakening their wall.

"Why are they doing that?" I asked. "They're making themselves vulnerable."

Malcolm kept silent, waiting for one of us to arrive at the answer.

"Their flanks," Aelric said. "They cannot allow our army to come around behind them. They need to match the length of our wall or exceed it."

Malcolm nodded, and we continued to watch as the Saxons lined up. Harold and the Thegns rode in front of them, shouting encouragement, giving directions. When the wall was solid, the army—as one massive unit—began marching up the rise toward the Vikings.

When the distance between them was no more than a hundred feet, Harold called them to a halt and rode forward, into the centre of the gap. Soon the shouts of the soldiers on each side were silenced as King Hardrada and Tostig rode out to meet him.

They were too far away to hear, but what they said was told to us later. First, Harold offered the Vikings mercy, after reminding them that they didn't deserve it. "You plundered my land and slaughtered my people," he shouted to them, "and yet I will spare your lives if you lay down your arms, return to your homeland and swear to never attack us again."

Tostig and King Hardrada conferred quietly, then Tostig addressed his brother. "And what gift do you give me in return for this favour?"

"If you give up this fight and swear fealty to me as your King, I will restore you as Earl of Northumbria," Harold replied.

"And what gift would you give King Hardrada, if he were to relinquish his claim to the English throne and return, empty handed, to Norway?"

Harold then asked what gift he would want.

"King Hardrada would require all the lands of Northumbria."

At that point, a cheer went up from the Viking ranks, which we heard even from that distance. I expect they could have heard it in York. When it subsided, Harold said. "If King Hardrada wants English land, I will provide six feet of it to bury him in. In fact, as he is so tall, I will grant him seven feet."

With that, Harold rode back to the Saxon line amid

the cheers and shouts of his soldiers.

At the time, we didn't know what had been said, but we knew it was a parley of some sort, an effort—however doomed—to avoid more bloodshed.

"Harold has shown wisdom," Malcolm said. "He offered his enemy something which they should desire above all—to avoid war. Having rejected it, Harold can now slaughter them without remorse, or mercy."

"Is that important?" Aelric asked.

"Very," Malcolm replied. "In battle, it may not save your life, but it may save your soul."

He turned to us then, looking at me, then Mitch and then Aelric, whose gaze he held.

"Tell me true, young Aelric, you were eager to taste battle and disappointed that I kept you back."

"I was ready to do my duty," Aelric said, standing straight and puffing out his chest.

"Then you must hear this, all of you." He stepped back from Aelric, looking at the three of us as he spoke.

"The death of another is not something to take lightly, and you must make the distinction between murder and killing, for when you murder a man, a bit of your soul dies with him. If you invade someone's home to steal their treasure and kill them, that is murder. However, if the owner of that house is able to fight off the intruder, or kill him to protect himself and his family, that is a just killing, and his conscience or his soul need not suffer. What Hardrada and Tostig are doing is the same thing, but on such a large scale, we call it war."

He paused, pointing toward the bodies, and the soldiers lining up across the river.

"Harold did not provoke this war. Hardrada and Tostig brought their armies here to murder and steal.

What you saw on that field—armed soldiers cutting down unarmed men—was not murder. Harold did not seek war, the Vikings did, and if you are unable to avoid battle, then you must do all you can to stop your enemy. Once you know you are in the right, take every advantage, every opportunity, use every trick and weapon at your disposal, for the sooner you defeat your foe, the sooner the killing will stop."

I wondered why he was telling us all this, and began to worry that he was planning to throw us into the battle after all. Then Mitch asked, "How do you know if you are in the right?"

"Just ask yourself, 'Am I able to walk away from this fight?' If you cannot, then you can fight, and kill, without remorse. If you can walk away, then you are the aggressor, and your soul is in danger."

A distant, pulsing thud caught our attention, and we turned to see the Saxon line begin to move, accompanied by the tramp of thousands of feet.

Malcolm stroked his beard. "Now the true battle begins. Watch and learn."

From the Saxon line, above the cacophony of clanking armour, clopping hooves, and the jeers of the Viking army, came a rhythmic thumping as the soldiers began striking the edges of their shields with the flat of their swords. The clang of metal on metal grew louder and louder until it drowned out every other sound. Along with it, in time with the beat of their swords, the Saxons began to chant. "Out! Out! Out!"

I turned to Malcolm. "What are they doing?"

But it was Aelric who answered. "It is our battle cry. A challenge to the enemy, and encouragement to themselves, to drive the invaders from their land."

The chanting and sword-beating continued as the

distance between the lines grew narrow until, with a deafening roar and a hellish clash of steel on steel, the slaughter began.

Almost instantly, the field on the far side of the river—once green and idyllic—became as blood-spattered as the near side. Saxons, Vikings, and horses fell. Swords, axes, shields, and severed limbs littered the ground that now ran red. And the screams of the dying filled the air.

Malcolm turned away and walked back toward the crest of the hill. We followed, glad to put the battle behind us. "There is little to gain in keeping watch," he said. "The plans, the posturing, the offers, and counteroffers have all been played out. It is now down to each man to kill or die, and those who know the skills of battle have the best chance of survival."

We reached the summit and continued down the far side, to where we had tied the horses. There, Malcolm retrieved his shield and held it out to Aelric. "It is now time for your final lesson."

Chapter 17

Mitch

"Hold them this way," Malcolm said.

We stood in a line, gripping our shields, trying to form a wall. Malcolm stood in front of us, setting the shields into position, interlocking them to form as solid a barrier as the three of us could manage. When we were in position, and our shields were locked as well as could be expected, he swung Aelric's axe at us, hitting the centre shield with the flat edge. The blow stung my arms and we staggered backward, but the little shield wall held.

He then had us form the wall again. And again. From sitting, from standing, from wandering the hillside. At Malcolm's call, we would rush together and lock our shields into place. And when we could do it perfectly, he had us do it again.

Then we practiced with the sword, with Malcolm showing us how to hold the shield to deflect the blows. He elected Aelric to swing the sword at him and each time he deflected the blow, causing Aelric to stumble as the heavy sword glanced off in a different direction.

"Now you," he said to Charlie, handing him his shield and the sword.

Malcolm watched, correcting his stance, showing him how to hold the sword and the axe, and how to strike with them, as well as defend from them.

When it was my turn, Charlie swung his sword at me so I could block it with the shield, and although the shock of the blow ran up my arm and through my shoulder like an electric jolt, I managed to deflect the blade, but I did drop the axe.

"But now what?" I asked. "I've avoided that blow, but I'm unarmed, fighting someone with a sword. What good is defence if you can't mount an offense?"

"If you are committed to battle," Malcolm said, "then you are always on the offense. You fight with everything you have, you take advantage any way you can, you find and use ways to fight your enemy that he will not expect."

"But how? I'm standing here in an empty field with nothing but a shield."

"You have provided the answer in your own question," Malcolm said. "Here, take my sword. Charlie, give me your shield."

I held the sword and shield ready, as I had been taught. Charlie and Aelric turned to watch. Malcolm raised his shield. "Now strike."

Feeling a little embarrassed, I swung as hard as I could. The next thing I knew I was on my back with Malcolm standing over me, the edge of the shield just touching my throat. Malcolm smiled down at me. "Just a shield?"

We practiced all that Malcolm taught us: how to use the momentum of the blow to bring the shield around and hit an attacker on his undefended side, how to use the edge of the shield as a blunt blade, capable of breaking bones and rendering an enemy immobile, and how to cut with the sword.

"Do not stab," he told us. "If you do, you will need to pull the blade out, and that takes precious time.

Swing the blade, cut and swipe at your enemy. Remember, you do not have to kill him, you only need to keep him from being able to kill you. A sliced upper arm, a gash across the chest, a cut to the leg, all these will stop an enemy, allowing you to move on."

We practiced under the blazing sun, as the day grew hotter, until, tired, hungry, and sore, we begged to stop. Malcolm said nothing. He simply led us to the crest of the hill and had us look down at the battle, where the significantly reduced Viking army and the slightly less reduced Saxon army were still grinding away at one another, stabbing, slashing, gouging, cleaving. The meadow was no longer a meadow but a pile of bloody bodies, Saxon and Viking. And, as in the earlier skirmish, the piles of bodies were not still, but writhing with the dying and wounded. Their cries for mercy or water joining the shouts of battle.

"Do you see these men resting?"

Then he led us back to the horses, where we continued to practice the art of war.

In time, Malcolm finally called a halt, and we sat on the grass, panting and gasping, wishing for water but knowing there was none to be had.

"Take courage, my young friends," Malcolm said. "Your trial will soon be over. But for now, we will return to the battle; it is time for the final act."

On the hilltop, we watched the battle, now a monotony of screams and gore and death, wondering how the soldiers continued to fight with no food or water. Incredibly, neither side had broken. The Viking shield wall—though stretched and thin in places—still held. Behind the wall, King Hardrada and Tostig rode back and forth, frantically pulling men from one place to move them to another where the wall threatened to break. But they were running out of time and men, and if the wall collapsed, the Vikings would be slaughtered.

Then the three messengers on horseback came galloping down the dusty road. Without hesitation they joined the battle as, behind them, the first of the Viking reinforcements arrived, led by another Viking warrior on horseback.

"That is the Viking chief Eystein Orri, the son-in-law of King Hardrada," Malcolm told us.

With Orri were dozens of Vikings, in full armour and carrying battle axes and shields. Soon, the dozens became hundreds as a flood of Viking warrior streamed onto the field. They joined the battle, shoring up the line, reinforcing the shield wall just as the exhausted Saxons were anticipating victory. Behind the Saxons, Harold and his Thegns rode, encouraging the men, but the Vikings, with fresh fighters, began to push the line back.

Aelric put his head in his hands. "It is over. We are doomed."

Malcolm put a hand on his shoulder. "You lose heart too quickly. True, the Viking numbers increase, but look closely at the new fighters."

We watched the road where the Vikings continued to pour in. The first of the fighters had been running and screaming war cries, but now they were walking, dragging themselves forward. Some fell to the ground and, only with great effort, rose to continue forward. Others remained where they fell.

"They were right to hurry to help their King," Malcolm said, "but their haste has cost them dearly. The Saxons may be disheartened for the moment, but if Harold can keep them in place, they will soon see that the fresh soldiers are more fatigued than they are.

And one can never discount the unexpected in war."

The battle had been raging for nearly four hours and the soldiers on each side were stooped and sluggish. Still, they slashed and stabbed at each other but not with the fervour they had displayed when the battle was first joined. The Saxon line was now matched in strength by the Viking shield wall, and it looked as if the bloody stalemate would continue until every man on the field was dead. Then the unexpected happened; King Hardrada, shouting exhortations to his rejuvenated army, suddenly fell silent as a Saxon arrow struck him in the throat.

Hardrada dropped his sword and grabbed at the arrow as blood gushed from the wound. Within seconds, he lay on the ground, dead.

Tostig assumed command, but soon, his voice, too, was silenced. Without a leader, the Vikings became disorganized, so Orri rushed into the battle, shouting orders and encouragement.

As the Viking shield wall began to collapse, Orri came forward, swinging a battle axe, screaming to the men to stand firm. The reinforcements Orri had led into the battle stood with him, fighting manically, but soon the final leader of the Viking army was gone, and the stalemate broke.

The Vikings retreated in disarray, charging down the road, to Riccal and their boats, pursued by the rejuvenated Saxons. The armies scrambled from the field, slipping over the blood and bodies, yelling and waving swords. The Saxons continued to cut down the Vikings as they ran and soon the dusty road was red with blood and littered with bleeding bodies.

As the shouts and the cries faded into the distance, we looked down at the battlefield. What should have been a silent and sombre place was now filled with the raucous cries of the ravens and crows, which were already beginning to gather in their hundreds.

After a minute of stunned silence, Malcolm turned away and led us back to the horses. "Tell me, my young friends, did you see any valour, any honour, any bravery that would entice you to do anything but avoid what you just witnessed?"

Charlie and I looked at one another. Aelric shook his head. "I saw brother facing brother, and a foreign king greedy for gold, and watched their ambitions kill thousands of innocent men."

Malcolm nodded. "The cause of all woes, large or small, can almost always be traced back to the desire for wealth, power, or revenge. Guard your soul, Aelric, that you may avoid these passions. Fight only to avoid fighting."

He turned to me and Charlie. "And what did you see today?"

Charlie stared at the ground. "I saw a flock of crows feasting on the dead."

"An appropriate image to keep in mind when the lure of war beckons."

"A flock of crows," I said. "Isn't that called a murder?"

Malcolm gave a wain smile. "Precisely."

Chapter 18

Charlie

After witnessing the battle, the calm of the camp, although it was buzzing with frantic activity, seemed surreal. The levy men and soldiers left behind to mind the camp were still busy building fires, erecting tents and gathering supplies, and as soon as we arrived, Malcolm put us to work.

"A hungry army is heading our way," he told them. "We had better prepare our defences."

Aelric helped us build the cooking fires, but then he begged Malcolm to let him return to his unit, leaving us to fetch water, cut vegetables and prepare the meat. I could tell he was shocked by what he had seen, and I understood his desire to be among people who were more familiar to him. It meant more work for us, but I was glad for it, because it helped me forget how stunned I was by what we had witnessed.

Soon the story of the battle began circulating as soldiers and levy men trickled back. Excitement grew as the tales, and the euphoria of victory, spread through the camp as thickly as the smell of wood smoke and roasting meat. The suckling pigs, legs of mutton, numerous chickens and many pots of stew were ready when the bulk of the army returned. Everyone cheered at the sight of Harold leading his tired but victorious soldiers. No one commented on how many were missing.

Celebrations erupted, barrels of ale, jugs of mead and wine skins appeared. Feasts were prepared for Harold and his Thegns, and the stew pots me and Mitch presided over began to empty. When there was none left, we cleaned the pots and started again.

More tales circulated, telling how the Saxons had chased the Vikings back to their boats, where Harold accepted a truce with King Hardrada's son, Olaf, in exchange for their oath to never attack England again. The defeated Vikings were then allowed to leave in their boats, filling only twenty-four of the three hundred they had arrived in.

"Those boats, their weapons, the armour, it's all there, lying near the river," a gleeful levy man told us as we lugged buckets of water from the river, "ripe for picking." Then he headed off in the direction of Riccal. Others followed, especially the levy men who had missed the battle entirely. They wanted to see for themselves and bring a souvenir back to their families to shore up tales of their own valour at the battle.

"Aren't they deserting?" I asked, as I watched another one go.

"More like AWOL," Mitch said, "but it sure isn't something they're supposed to do."

I picked up my bucket. "No one seems to mind."

Mitch, struggling with his own bucket, ran a hand across his brow. "I suppose they're too busy celebrating."

As the evening drew in more fires were lit and the grateful citizens of York came to the camp, bringing more food and drink. The laughter and the cheers grew more raucous and were now interspersed with the delighted squeals of young girls, giddy with euphoria at being in the presence of such brave soldiers. Me and Mitch were kept busy fetching meat and beer for the soldiers, which was hard work after our long and tiring day. The only good thing was, we hadn't run into Reinhart or any of his men, and I, at least, was harbouring a secret hope that they might not have returned from the battle. But then, as we passed by a campfire surrounded by soldiers and giggling women, a familiar voice rang out.

"Look who's here, my cooks."

In the centre of the group of soldiers, sat Reinhart and his companions. They were filthy and blood-spattered, their hair plastered to their heads with dried sweat. Blood seeped from a bulky bandage around Hoban's arm, dripping onto the tunic of the pretty red-haired girl sitting on his knee. The other soldiers and girls turned to stare at us.

"Staying here to do woman's work while men go to fight," Gerwald said, his voice thick. "I should execute you for desertion right here and now."

The soldiers snickered; the girls giggled.

"We were ordered to stay," I said. "Someone had to mind the camp."

"And feed you," Mitch added.

Reinhart jumped to his feet, knocking the girl who had been sitting on his lap onto the ground. "And that someone was not to be you," he shouted, pointing a finger at us. "You were meant to be in the middle of that battle. Mercenaries? You're cowards. And you have no business among these brave men."

The soldier shouted their agreement while the women laughed and clapped.

"Get out of my camp. Sleep outside in the field, that's the place for cowards."

"You're in the wrong camp," one of the soldiers snickered. "This is the hero's camp."

"And take your friends with you," said another. "Make a coward's camp. You can all sleep there."

The soldiers stamped their feet and cheered, shouting their ascent.

"But who's going to bring you food and tend your fires if you send us all away?" Mitch asked.

"We have real women to serve us," Reinhart shouted. "Brave men will not be served by cowards."

Reinhart drew his sword. Hoban, Blekwulf, Gerwald and the other soldiers followed suit. "Come on, men," he said. "We've rid our land of Vikings, now let's rid our camp of cowards."

The small band of soldiers surged forward, dragging me and Mitch through the camp, gathering rowdy followers as they sought out all the levy men who had not fought in the battle. One of the first unfortunates was Aelric, grabbed by a soldier as he sat by a fire with half a dozen others. He and his friends were shoved into the growing knot of people and pushed along with us.

"What's going on?" he asked.

"We got Reinhart angry again," Mitch said.

"What did you do?"

"We let him see us," I said.

Soon, nearly a hundred confused levy men were marched to the outskirts of the camp.

"Here," Reinhart said. "This is your camp."

The bewildered men grumbled. "We're in the middle of a field," one of them said.

Reinhart smiled. "Yes, it is more than you deserve, but it will suffice."

The soldiers, still holding ale mugs and women,

roared with laughter. Then, with the joke over, they began to wander crookedly back to camp. The man who had protested now stood in front of Reinhart. "You can't do this to us," he said. "We serve in the same army, we follow the same King, you can't banish us."

Reinhart hit him with the hilt of his sword. "Do not think to question me," he shouted at the man now lying in the grass at his feet. Then he turned to me and Mitch. "This is your camp now. Do not return to ours."

Then he, too, left. The stricken man rose to his feet, helped by a few of his friends. The rest of the group folded their arms across their chests, shook their heads and kicked at the grass, muttering, and scowling at us.

"They blame you," Aelric said.

"So do I," I said.

Gradually, the men began to settle in, making the most of the situation. Some sneaked back into the camp for blankets, food, and firewood. Others returned to gather up their souvenir weapons and shields to keep them safe. Soon they had built a row of fires with a few sagging tents along each side and, between the tents, mounds of dry grass and hay for the less fortunate.

Aelric, too, made a stealthy visit to the main camp and returned with our shields, blankets, and Malcolm, who brought food.

"I heard of your misfortune," he said. "You are lucky; Reinhart is a man quick to anger. In his present state, he might have killed you instead of banishing you. But now that you are out of his sight, endeavour to remain so."

We built our fire at the edge of the group, and piled

dry grass for sleeping mats. Then, as full dark settled and the stars shone bright, we sat around our fire and ate. Malcolm had brought more food and drink than we could eat, so we shared it among the others, which didn't earn their good will but at least made them stop scowling at us.

Disappointingly, Malcolm was unable to remain long, and had left as soon as he had handed over the sacks of provisions. "I must return to camp," he'd told us. "I had hoped this night to tell you more of the talisman, and of things you need to know, but now is not the time." He gazed around at the flickering fires and the growing darkness. "But perhaps this is for the better. I sense a change. Be ready for it."

Then he had walked away, back toward the main camp, which was barely visible in the distance.

"We should sleep now," Aelric said after we had eaten. "They were happy to banish us tonight, but they will be here for us early to clean up the camp after the night's revelry."

We prepared our makeshift beds, keeping as close to the fire as we dared, staying just far enough away so our beds didn't catch fire. As we settled in, Mitch said, "Did any of you notice if there were any sentries?"

Aelric sat up. "No, I did not."

"They're making the same mistake the Vikings did," I said.

"But there isn't a Viking within a hundred miles of here," Aelric said.

Mitch considered a moment. "Still, shouldn't we post some guards, just in case?"

Aelric gave a short laugh and pointed toward the rest of the camp. "Would you like to tell them they need to go on guard duty?"

"No," Mitch said, getting to his feet. "I'll do it myself."

He bent to pick up his shield, but Aelric laid his hand on it. "No, you get some sleep. I'll take the first watch."

He took his axe and walked through the camp, to the curious stares of the levy men. None followed; they all retired or remained sitting around their fires, talking softly amongst themselves.

Chapter 19

Mitch

A sliver of moon shone in the dark sky when Aelric return hours later. Charlie and I dragged ourselves from the warmth of our blankets and sat shivering on the ground, stirring the embers of the fire.

"All quiet," Aelric said, as he pulled his blanket around his shoulders. "Except for the occasional soldier stumbling into the fields to relieve himself. I would stand a little further away from camp if I were you. Though I expect they should mostly be asleep by now."

With that he turned and fell asleep himself, his axe still clutched in his hand.

Charlie and I took our shields and walked into the cold night.

We found the flattened pathway cutting through the field that marked the main access to the camp and stood shivering in the waist high weeds, one on either side of it, our backs to the camp, looking at the emptiness beyond.

"What are we supposed to be looking for?" Charlie whispered.

"I don't know," I said. "Trouble, I guess."

"Do you think we'll see any?"

"No, but that just means we're in for a boring night, and that will make it harder to stay awake."

"Well, stamp your feet occasionally," Charlie said. "Or walk in circles. That will help keep you awake."

It seemed a good plan, but almost immediately my eyelids grew heavy, and I saw that Charlie was not holding his shield so much as he was leaning on it. Every time I blinked, my eyes stayed closed for longer and longer, and soon I found myself sitting on the ground, with no memory of how I got there. But it was comfortable, and it felt good to rest. I closed my eyes, listening to the sounds of the night, feeling the chill breeze against my skin. Peaceful, so peaceful.

With a jolt, my eyes snapped open. Had I been asleep? I didn't think so, but I had been on the verge. In the black sky, the crescent moon now hung closer to the horizon. I had been asleep, but something had awakened me.

I sat up cautiously and looked over to where Charlie was supposed to be and saw nothing but weeds. I held my breath and strained to hear above the pounding of my heart. Then I heard it, the sound of men moving. Whoever it was, there were a lot of them, and they were coming toward the camp. Not at a run or quick march, but slowly, stealthily. I raised my head above the weeds but could see nothing. Quietly as I could, I crawled from the weeds onto the broad flattened path and, taking one last look toward the sound of the approaching men, dashed to the other side. Charlie was lying on the ground, asleep, and in my hurry to get out of sight, I tripped over him. Charlie moaned and sat up.

"Ow, hey! What the—"

I held a finger to my lips and crawled to him.

"Out there," I whispered.

"Where?"

I pointed.

"I don't see anything."

"Wait."

Then, out on the dark plain, the shadows began to move. Men, a hundred or more, walking slowly, silently. An array of swords, shields and battle axes glinted in the starlight.

"They're heading for our camp," Charlie whispered. "We have to do something."

"If we move, they'll see us. Keep still."

We held our breath as the men approached.

"They're Vikings," I said, barely breathing the words into Charlie's ear. Charlie nodded, watching the small army that was now directly in front of us.

The lead Viking raised his arm. Those behind immediately dropped to a crouch.

"I heard something," the leader said.

We froze, but then another Viking came from the direction of the camp. He wore no armour and carried no weapons and ran, stooping low, in near silence.

"What have you found?" the leader asked.

"They sleep, heavy with drink, the soldiers, their women, their servants. And those who are awake are too drunk to fight."

The leader clapped a hand on the man's shoulder. "This is good. We can attack the camp and kill them as they sleep. By the time an alarm is raised, thousands will be dead."

"There is another camp," the man said.

"Another?"

The man looked in the direction of our small camp, hidden in the darkness. "Yes, and I don't know what to make of it." Then he fell silent.

"Well make something of it," the leader said

harshly.

"They are near our number, armed and taking no part in the celebrations. They could be outcasts, or—"

"Or the English suspect our plans," the leader said. "Sober warriors, waiting for our attack. If we go to the camp, they will come from behind and cut us down."

"I don't know if they are warriors," the man said. "They are not keeping watch. They all appear to be asleep."

"Then whoever they are, we kill them first."

He signalled for the men behind him to keep low. With hardly a sound, the Vikings moved from the road into the field, tramping over the spot where, until recently, I had been sleeping, following the man who had spied out our camp

"Run to the main camp," I said as soon as the last Viking disappeared into the night. "See if you can wake any of the soldiers. I'll run to our camp and warn them."

Together we charged toward the main camp, our shields thumping on our backs. As we drew near, I turned to head toward our camp, but then we both stopped and froze on the spot. The shadow of a man stood in the field not far from us. We crouched together in the weeds, panting.

"Was that a Viking or a Saxon?" Charlie asked.

"I don't know."

"Do you think he saw us?"

I didn't have the opportunity to answer. Heavy hands fell on me, gripping the back of my neck and pulling me to my feet.

"Ha, just as I suspected," Reinhart sneered. "When I heard you were on guard duty, I knew I'd find you either sleeping or deserting."

Charlie stood, and Reinhart gripped him with his free hand. "We weren't deserting," Charlie squeaked. "There are men out there. Armed Vikings, sneaking toward our camp."

Reinhart shook him like a terrier shaking a rat. "Fancy stories. Is that the best you can do to try to save your necks? It's the axe for you, and there's no Falan here to protect you, and that meddling Malcolm with his pagan potions can't save you this time."

Reinhart started toward our camp, dragging us with him as we struggle to stay on our feet. He held me in an iron grip, even as he swayed and stumbled from side to side.

"Faster," I said. "We don't have much time."

"In a hurry to meet the executioner's block?"

"No, you idiot," Charlie said. "We're in a hurry to save their lives."

"Watch your tongue you little whelp," Reinhart bellowed. He threw Charlie to the ground and, still holding onto me, drew his sword. "I'll have your head for that, here and now."

Charlie's eyes widened as the blade arced downward. He rolled away, onto his stomach, and the blade smashed into his shield, and the shield smashed into his back. It must have knocked the wind out of him, but he scrambled to his hands and knees, lurching forward. I heard the whoosh of the blade again and saw it pass a hair's breadth from the back of his neck. Then he was on his feet, out of Reinhart's range.

"Get back here and face your punishment," Reinhart said, dragging me along as he lunged forward. Charlie ran further, keeping out of his reach. "I'll kill your brother if you don't come back."

Charlie hesitated. Reinhart smiled and raised his

sword.

"No, Charlie," I said. "Run!"

Charlie ran.

Chapter 20

Charlie

It wasn't an easy choice, but I knew Mitch was right: if I stayed, Reinhart would kill us both, and the enemy would kill the levy men and take Harold's army by surprise. If I could get to our camp in time, they might be saved, and if Mitch could stay alive that long, he might be saved too. It sounded cowardly, but running away was our only chance, so I ran, faster than I had ever run before.

The shield jolted on my shoulder, my back burned where Reinhart's sword had hit me, and every muscle in my body ached. But still I ran.

Behind me, I heard Reinhart shouting, and Mitch shouting in return. That was a good sign; as long as Reinhart kept shouting, he wouldn't be using his sword.

The dim lights from the smouldering fires drew nearer. Then the shouting stopped, replaced by the clash of metal on metal. I ran faster.

Chapter 21

Mitch

"Your brother is a coward," Reinhart said. There was a note of triumph in his voice. "He abandoned you rather than face his punishment like a man."

"He didn't abandon me. He's trying to warn the camp. It's our only chance. Take me to the camp. You'll see."

"Drag you all the way to the camp? You're not worth it. I said I'd kill you here and I mean to."

"What good will that do?" I said, panic rising in my voice. "If you take me to the camp, you can make an example of me, like you did to the deserter. You can make an example of both of us, just take me to the camp."

Reinhart paused. "For a dead man, you make a good argument," he said. "But I think otherwise. I will make an example of your brother. He will die before the entire company, after I tell them how he ran like a girl from danger and let his brother take his punishment. He will die in shame. And you will die knowing you have been betrayed by your own blood."

I felt my feet leave the ground as Reinhart lifted me by the neck. Then he threw me as easily as I would throw a doll. I landed in the tall grass, winded and stunned. Then I saw Reinhart standing above me, raising his sword.

Chapter 22

Charlie

I raced into the camp. All was quiet. Everyone was asleep, some in makeshift tents, others huddled under blankets and lying on piles of hay. I ran to Aelric and shook him by the shoulder. "Wake up."

Aelric's eyes opened. "Wha …"

"Get up!" I hissed. "We're under attack. Armed men, Vikings, heading this way."

Aelric stumbled out of bed and grabbed his axe. "Where? Are you sure?"

"Quiet! They're close. They mean to kill us all in our sleep."

"Then we must flee."

"No. They're close. If they hear us running away, they'll be on us in a moment. We need to stop them here; we have to stop them from getting into the main camp."

Aelric looked around uncertainly. "What will we do?"

I scanned the camp, trying to focus my thoughts. It was flat land with no barriers or high ground to use to our advantage. "Wake everyone, as quickly and quietly as you can. The Vikings mustn't know we're on to them. Form a line just behind the fires."

"But what—"

"Do it. And bring all the weapons you can."

Grabbing a stick, I ran down the line, from fire to fire, stirring the embers until they glowed. Behind me, I heard urgent whispers as Aelric woke the levy men. As more and more men assembled, I snatched up their bedding and threw it down behind the fires. "Help me," I said to the bewildered men close by. "Make a line of hay bundles behind the fires. Then have everyone line up with their shields and whatever weapons they have."

They obeyed without question, too frightened to argue. Soon a ragged line of men, most holding the shields and swords they had taken from the Vikings, stood behind the glowing fire pits and in front of the hay. They all, even Aelric, looked at me, bewildered.

"Crouch low," I said, whispering as loudly as I dared. I raced up and down the line, telling the men to make a shield wall. They looked at me quizzically, so I grabbed a shield from the nearest man and gave it to Aelric. "Take that side of the line. I'll take this side. Show them how to lock their shields but stay low until the Vikings arrive. When I give the signal throw the hay into the fire pits. And then stand firm."

I ran down the line. Nearly seventy men with shields. Would it hold? At my end of the line a group of unarmed levy men waited. "Everyone without shields leave. Now. Hide in the dark outside the camp. When the battle begins, attack them from behind."

"With what?" one of the men asked.

"With anything," I said, already turning away. I slotted myself into the line, showed the men next to me how to properly lock their shields together and then, as a single unit, we crouched in the dark and waited.

Chapter 23

Mitch

I tried to roll the way Charlie had but managed to only turn halfway when the sword bit into the ground by my side. I scrambled to my feet, but Reinhart kicked me, sending me sprawling into the grass. I turned, saw the sword streaking toward me and held my shield up. The blow shook my entire body, and the clang of metal left my ears ringing. I moved backward, hampered by the shield but not daring to drop it. Another blow knocked me flat on the ground.

"I should have killed you the moment I saw you," Reinhart said from above.

A blow landed on the shield again. It bucked in my hands, but I held tight, trying to fit my entire body under it. "You soft little whelps!" Another blow. "Playing soldier with your fine shields, and your fancy cloak." Reinhart struck again, a hard blow, but not lethal, not enough to knock the shield from my grip and cleave me in two. Reinhart was toying with me, like a giant cat, enjoying watching his prey quiver in fear. "I don't know who you are." The shield rang as Reinhart's sword struck again. "I don't know what you are." And again. "Or why you're here." And again. "But I'm putting an end to it right now." Reinhart's final blow knocked the shield from my grip as if Reinhart was batting away a fly.

I lay on the ground, winded, defenceless with Reinhart standing over me, his sword raised high above his head.

Chapter 24

Charlie

The Vikings entered the camp swiftly but stealthily, slashing through the tents, stabbing into the discarded blankets, knocking everything aside as they came. Then, as they slowly began to realize the camp was empty, they stopped and looked uncertainly at their leader.

"Now!" I shouted.

Each man grabbed a mound of hay and flung it to the ground in front of the line. Then they stood and locked their shields into a wall. The startled Vikings stepped back, staring at the line of warriors that appeared out of nowhere until the rising smoke obscured them from view.

I hadn't counted on the smoke. My eyes stung and my throat burned and, even worse, I couldn't see what the Vikings were doing. Then, from down the line, a rhythmic thumping started, followed by a low chant that grew stronger and bolder with each beat. It spread up the line until every man, including me, was beating the side of his shield and shouting, "Out! Out! Out!"

With a blood-curdling scream, the Vikings charged.

Chapter 25

Mitch

The sword hovered in the air, halted by the sound of the distant scream. Then the sound of battle reached us.

Reinhart said nothing. He turned and ran toward the main camp, leaving me gasping for breath and running my hands over my neck to make sure I was still alive, and my head was still attached to my body. Then I sat up. The attack had begun. Charlie was there. I grabbed my shield and ran.

Chapter 26

Charlie

The men braced themselves, but as the Vikings slammed into them, they staggered back, our thin wall already crumbling. We scrambled to reform before the Vikings had a chance to breech our ranks.

"Hold the line," I shouted, struggling to push back against the human tide.

Slashing and shouting, our line slowly inched backward.

"There's too many of them," a man next to me screamed.

"Hold on," I shouted. "Just a few more seconds."

Then the smouldering hay exploded into flame, leaping up into the Viking ranks. The pressure on our line went suddenly slack as the Vikings screamed. Those in the flames tried to pull back, tumbling into the men behind them. Those in front lurched forward to escape the flames, cutting themselves off from the others, making them easy targets for the levy men.

The attack wavered just long enough for us to reform the wall. As the flames and smoke abated, I saw, behind the front line, Vikings running with their clothing in flames, others writhing on the ground and some lying still in the grass, smoke rising from their charred bodies.

The Vikings charged again, but this time they were

less certain, and the levy men were more confident. The clash shook the wall, but it held fast and then the slaughter began.

In hand-to-hand combat, the levy men lost their advantage. With no combat skills, they were easy prey for the Viking warriors. I grabbed a sword from a fallen man and tried to put my recent training to use. My attempts were futile. All I could do was use my shield to ward off as many blows as I could before I was struck down.

Where the hell was the rear attack?

Chapter 27

Mitch

I rushed toward the chaos of the battle and found a cluster of levy men standing outside the camp, watching.

"What the hell are you doing?" I shouted.

The men looked at me. "We're supposed to attack from behind. But we don't know ... we've got no one to tell us ..."

"Follow me."

I ran around the tangle of battling men, leading the band of farmers, armed with rakes, hoes, and scythes, behind the Vikings. I charged toward them, hoping I was being followed, but with no time to look back. Charlie was in there and I had to help him. Gripping my shield in front of me, I leapt onto the back of a Viking and brought the metal edge down hard on the back of his neck. The man crumpled like an empty sack. Then I grabbed the fallen man's sword and turned to the men behind me.

"Come on!"

With a shout, the men rushed forward, slashing out with whatever was in their hands, others grabbing weapons from the fallen, and together we pressed the attack.

When the Vikings saw they were being attacked from behind, they turned to face the new threat. But now they were a thin line fighting an enemy on two sides. And the levy men on the shield wall had the advantage.

I pulled the men back and struck another part of the line. By now most of the men had shields, swords and axes and the Vikings found the fight on either side to be equally treacherous as we skirmished with unsuspecting Vikings in different parts of the line. One man next to me, a farmer, still fought with his scythe, arcing it over his head to strike from above, taking one Viking at a time.

"No," I shouted to him. "Use it like you're cutting wheat. Sweep along their legs."

The man grinned and turned the scythe around, sweeping a wide arc that sliced through the thighs of half a dozen Vikings. They fell in a heap, screaming, writhing, and spouting blood. Some crawled forward, still waving their axes until they were stopped. Another levy man who had dropped his scythe in favour of a sword now grabbed it up and began cutting into the Viking line. Enraged, the Vikings turned on us. I stood back-to-back with the few remaining levy men, inside a tiny circular shield wall, surrounded by Vikings.

Chapter 28

Charlie

I felt the wall beginning to break, but then the onslaught eased off. I was dimly aware of confusion in the back of the Viking line.

"The counter-attack has started," I yelled. "Move forward"

Encouraged, the men locked the shield wall tighter and inched the increasingly confused Vikings back to the original line, forcing them to fight while standing on the hot coals of the fire pits.

Here we held, shouting, and swinging our swords as the Vikings alternated between one threat and the other.

I sensed the shape of the battle changing. It was no longer two lines but turning into a cluster of skirmishes. I moved the men near me forward and saw Aelric was moving his end of the line up as well. We were outflanking the Vikings, and now the fight turned into a deadly symphony of clashing steel.

Chapter 29

Mitch

I fought for my life, warding off blows with my shield and thrusting with the sword. Around me, men screamed and fell, and the trampled grass beneath my feet became slick with blood. The lines grew thin but still we battled on. The cluster of levy men struggled to break free of the encircling Vikings, clashing one-on-one in a desperate, bloody bid for freedom. I tried to fall back but stumbled over a body. A Viking charged me, his axe raised. I scrambled to raise my shield but knew it was too late. Then the Viking fell dead beside me, struck from behind by a levy man who had found a spear. I jumped to my feet and turned toward a new threat, clashing shield to shield with another warrior. I raised my sword. I saw my opponent's raised axe. Then I stopped.

"Aelric?"

"Mitch?"

"Look out!"

We locked our shields to face the new threat, then called for the men around us to reform the wall. The Vikings were now virtually surrounded and their numbers few. The battle had turned against them, but they fought madly. I wished we could offer them a chance to surrender, or at least ease up the attack, but I recalled the Viking on the bridge, and what I had overheard them planning for us, so the fight continued. It was gruelling and gruesome and, one by one, the Vikings fell until there was not a single one left standing.

Chapter 30

Charlie

We stood together, me, Mitch, Aelric and the remaining levy men, panting, shaking, and staring around at the sight surrounding us. As far as we could see into the dark night, bodies lay, both Viking and Saxon. In the gloom the wounded screamed and moaned, and the smell of blood became overpowering.

One of the levy men turned to us. "What are we to do now?"

Others also turned our way and we saw they had accepted us as their leaders. Though I didn't feel like leading, I knew I had to say something. Then, in the distance, I saw a line of torches coming our way.

"Another attack?" someone asked.

"No," Mitch said. "They came from the camp. I think that's our reinforcements."

They arrived moments later, Reinhart and a band of soldiers—some staggering, all bleary-eyed—their weapons ready. They stared, open-mouthed, at what they found. Even Reinhart was speechless.

The soldiers set to work, dispatching the wounded Vikings, collecting their own and transporting them back to camp. Soon the field was silent and still.

The levy men rooted through what remained of our camp, gathering their meagre possessions.

"I wonder if we'll need to build another camp,"

Mitch said, shaking out his blanket. "Or if we'll be allowed back in the main camp now."

I shook my head. "What, Reinhart rescind one of his orders?"

"But if he leaves us here," Aelric said, "he will look dishonourable to the others."

"Then I think he has a dilemma on his hands," Mitch said.

The men, their possessions piled by their feet, waited while Reinhart busied himself with his soldiers. The stalemate was cut short by the arrival of another group from camp.

These soldiers came on horseback, their armour gleaming in the torchlight. From their midst rode a tall man wearing a helmet and chain mail. He dismounted and approached the band of levy men. As he got near, he removed his helmet. A gasp rose from the soldiers. Aelric leaned close. "That's King Harold," he whispered.

Around us, men fell to their knees—levy men, soldiers, even Reinhart and his men—so we did the same.

"Are you the men who saved my army?" Harold asked. The levy men around us nodded.

"You have shown yourselves brave and worthy. I am in your debt. Rise, all of you. You will stay in my camp."

He ordered those with him to take the men and their belongings to the royal tents at the centre of the camp. Me and Mitch slung our shields and Aelric picked up his axe. Together we followed the levy men. Then one of Harold's men stopped me and Mitch. "The King wishes to speak with you."

With regret, we parted from Aelric, and watched the

levy men follow the horses into the night, as we were led to where Harold waited. The king gazed at us, stroking his short beard. "Did they tell me true? Are you the ones who led the attack?"

We nodded. "Yes," we said in unison. Then Mitch added. "Your highness."

"Yet my Thegns tell me that you are simple levy men, cooks for the Sussex regiment." He turned to Reinhart, who was idling nearby. "How has this been allowed to happen? And why were these men camped out here?"

Reinhart bowed to the king. "My Lord, I … they…"

"We were guarding the camp," Mitch said. "Our commander thought we needed alert and rested men to serve as sentries. We volunteered."

"Is this true?"

Reinhart bowed again. "It is."

Harold, his shaggy eyebrows raised, looked from Reinhart to Mitch and then to me. "You have done well. But I would know more about your cooks." He stepped close, peering down at us. "I have heard … rumours. You will dine with me. I will send for you."

He mounted his horse then, and with a final look at the carnage, led his men back toward the camp.

Reinhart continued to stare at us, his fists clenched, his face growing dark. "You dare speak to the King on my behalf? And now you have the King's favour. Don't let it comfort you; I will be watching."

Then he left and began barking orders to his men.

When we arrived, bone-tired and aching, at the main camp, the eastern sky was beginning to glow with the promise of dawn. We expected the camp to be silent, but many soldiers were awake, not drinking and revelling, but talking quietly around their fires. When they saw us, they cheered. Some ran to us, slapping us so hard on our back that we nearly stumbled. All we could do was smile and return the soldier's enthusiastic gestures with weary waves. "I feel like an idiot," I said.

"Just keep walking."

We went to Malcolm's camp and found him sitting by a fire over a steaming pot. He looked up as we came near, a tight smile on his face. "And how fare you, my young adventurous friends?"

We flopped down next to the fire.

"You heard."

"All have heard. But I more than others." He began scooping thick stew into bowls. "You used your training well."

"Did you know this was going to happen," Mitch asked. "Is that why you took us to the battle?"

Malcolm placed the bowls next to us. "I saw an opportunity. And knowledge is never wasted. But this ordeal has passed. You need food now, and rest."

"But the King—" I said.

Malcolm held up his hand. "Yes, the King. You are to dine with him. Do not worry. That will not be until this evening."

"How do you—"

"Eat. Then sleep. Then we talk. There is much for you to learn about the Talisman."

Chapter 31

Mitch

For the first time since we arrived, we didn't have to march, or work, or fight. The army, too, remained in the camp, resting and celebrating, though the level of revelry dropped as the day wore on.

Charlie and I slept into the afternoon and woke groggy and sore. Malcolm gave us food and, as we sat at the fire and ate. Passing soldiers called to us and we raised our ale mugs in reply, never letting on that they were filled with goat's milk that Malcolm had managed to find.

Once again, the sun shone bright in a cloudless sky. Though not as hot as the previous day, it was warm enough to tempt us into joining some soldiers and levy men swimming in a nearby river. We returned in the late afternoon, refreshed, and feeling far removed from the horrors of the previous day.

As twilight approached, Malcolm built up the fire and we sat around it, watching the flames flicker in the gathering dark.

"Harold will send for you soon," Malcolm said. "It is time to talk of the Talisman."

"Is it lost?" I asked. "Like last time?"

Malcolm shook his head. "No, it is safe. It resides in the Sacred Tor. As long as it remains in place, the Land will be safe, and no invader will have a chance of success."

"That's why you weren't worried about the outcome of the battle," Charlie said. "You knew King Harold couldn't lose."

"He benefits from the protection of the Talisman," Malcolm said. "But it does not protect him directly; it protects the Land. Still, it is a formidable advantage."

"He's still alive though," Charlie said. "And the Vikings have been defeated." He looked around. "So, there's nothing else to worry about."

"Except getting our cloak back," I reminded him.

There was silence for a few moments, then Charlie jumped to his feet, suddenly excited. "With all this celebrating going on," he said, "we could easily sneak into Falan's tent and take it back."

"We could do it tonight," I said, also rising. "After dinner."

"The sooner the better. We've done what we came to do; there's no reason to stay."

Malcolm, however, wasn't sharing our excitement. He continued to sit, staring into the fire. "I fear your enthusiasm is misplaced," he said. "What you plan will be harder than you think, and the danger to the Land is just beginning."

Charlie and I sat.

Malcolm stared into the fire for a long time, then said, "It is true I came to find you on that day. Had you been there, we would have travelled to the Sacred Tor and stood guard over the Talisman. But once the levy was recalled, I had no choice but to go with Reinhart."

"But the other guy," Charlie said.

Malcolm held up a hand to silence him. "Lubbik," he said. "Another, like myself, the only other who knows the secrets of the Talisman. I had thought him safely in the west with the Talisman, but your story confirms that he is here, and I fear that is not a good omen. He may be thinking of bringing the Talisman to Harold, which would be a grave mistake, or he may be conspiring to give it to William, which would be treason. Either way, he must not know I am here. If he feels safe, he will take no rash action."

"He's that old guy with Falan," Charlie said, "isn't he?"

"The one who convinced Falan to take our cloak from Reinhart," I added.

Malcolm nodded. "Reinhart merely coveted your cloak. But Lubbik knows what it is, and now Lord Falan knows as well. Taking it back from Reinhart would have been difficult; getting it from Lord Falan will be impossible."

"But there has to be some way to get at it," I said. "Because the alternative is to stay here forever."

"All in good time," Malcolm said. "But first we need to see off the final threat."

"Didn't we?"

"The Vikings were a formidable foe, but they were never the main threat. William of Normandy covets the crown, and he will soon make his move."

"But Aelric told us they waited for William's attack all summer and he never came," Charlie said.

"And that is what worries me. I fear he was waiting for something."

"What?"

"You."

Charlie stared. His mouth open but he seemed unable to speak.

"We … us?" I said. "Why?"

"The Talisman is not unknown among the royalty

153

of these lands. Tales of its power have come through the ages. Tales of a mighty army of knights who will rise at its bidding to defend the Land. Tales William knows well. His roots are in this land. He believes in the Talisman, and in the legends of the knights. In fact, he is counting on them."

"If he knows he can't win, why is he even trying?"

"He believes the Talisman's power resides with he who possesses it. Whoever owns the Talisman cannot be defeated. So, his only hope is to secure the Talisman for himself."

"He's going to steal it?"

"I believe so. William has spies, even here. They are waiting for the right moment to send a message to William, and I believe that moment has arrived. It was never a matter of sending an invading army to steal the Talisman. Though many know of the Talisman, few know where it is hidden, and fewer still hold the knowledge of how to access it. William waited, content to let Harold weaken his army fighting Tostig and Hardrada. He knew they could not win as long as the Talisman remained in place. But now that the Vikings have been defeated, he is looking for his moment. When news reaches him that the cloak has been found and the knights of old have, indeed, returned to defend the Land, he will sail his army to England, and send his spies to take the Talisman."

"What do we have to do with all this?"

"Harold, too, knows of the Talisman. He basks in its protection. Soon, he will have you at his table. He wants to know if you are truly the knights of legend. There will be others there, and they, too, will be interested in what you have to say."

"What do we say?"

"The truth. But take note of Falan, his interest in your story, and your cloak. And remember, Harold has many enemies, trust no one."

"Will any of this help us get our cloak back?"

"It may. It must. And not merely for your sake. It is true that the cloak brings you to where you are needed and returns you home, but it is also the key to the Talisman. For only a Guardian of the Talisman, in rightful possession of the cloak, can access the Talisman's Temple. This is why you have gained the notice of Harold, and William. Where you are, so is the cloak, and so is access to the Talisman."

Malcolm's voice grew quiet as heavy footsteps approached.

"Our time is short, and we may not have a chance to speak of this again. Mark my words; wait, watch, you will know when it is time to act. And now, I believe your escorts are here."

We looked up as six armed soldiers strode into the camp. Their leader, bearded and grim-faced, stood over us. "King Harold desires that you dine with him this night. Make yourselves ready."

I looked at Charlie. "But we are ready."

The soldier wrinkled his nose in disgust. "You are wearing rags."

"These are our clothes," Charlie said, standing straight and looking into the leader's eyes. "If Harold won't have us wearing these, then we will not go."

The soldier blinked, a look of unpleasant surprise on his face. "Follow," he said. Then he turned sharply and left, with his men trailing after him. Malcolm nodded in answer to our questioning glances, and we followed.

Chapter 32

Charlie

The soldiers marched on either side of us, as if we were prisoners in danger of escape. They marched us through the camp, to the outer circle of royal tents, where the levy men who had fought off the Vikings were now staying. When they recognized us, they shouted and cheered, and we waved, feeling embarrassed, like we were visiting royalty or something. The soldiers didn't wave. They marched, looking straight ahead.

We marched past them, to the inner circle of tents spaced tightly together. The tent we entered was not only the largest in the circle, it was the largest in the camp, tall and wide as a small house, supported by thick wooden beams, with a flag flying from a pole protruding from the peaked roof. Two guards pulled the entrance flaps back, allowing us, and the soldiers accompanying us, to enter.

Inside, the packed earth was covered with plush carpet, the walls hung with tapestries, and torches stood at intervals, filling the spacious room with light and smoke. A long table stood in the centre, lit by candles, making the plates, cups, knives, and bowls glimmer in the flickering light. Twenty chairs surrounded it, and at the far end, in the largest, most ornate chair, sat Harold, dressed in scarlet robes, and flanked by a bevy of servants. As we entered, the soldiers stopped and stepped away from us. I tried to stand straight and struggled not to cough in the suddenly smoky air.

Harold rose. Beneath his robe, he wore a sword, and there was a dagger tucked into his belt. "Greetings. Come and sit."

He dismissed the soldiers with a wave of his hand, and we approached the table uncertainly.

"My esteemed guests," Harold said, "do not be shy. Sit here, by me."

He indicated two smaller chairs close to his left. We sat, and I noticed as I did, that although there were many dishes on the table, there was no food. Not even a glass of water.

"Thank you for inviting us," Mitch said. Leave it to him to remember—even in such unbelievable circumstances—to be polite.

"Yeah," I said, following his lead. "We're honoured."

"The honour is mine," Harold said. Then he leaned forward and spoke low, as if to share a secret with us. "Even a king is humbled in the presence of greatness."

"What are you talking about?"

Harold sat up and straightened his robes. "In good time. Our other guests arrive."

The tent flaps parted again, pulled aside by unseen hands, and a group of men entered. Their fine clothes and flowing cloaks identified them as Thegns. One of them, wearing tight pants, a floppy hat, and a fancy doublet that looked like it was made of red satin, was Lord Falan.

Without thinking, I jumped to my feet, pointing. "That's the man ... he's got ..."

Harold put a hand on my shoulder and gently, but firmly, pushed me back into my seat. I thought Harold would be angry, but when I looked at him, he was smiling. "All in good time," he said. Then he stood and spread his arms in welcome, showing his dagger and sword. "Greetings my friends. Come. Sit. Eat."

The Thegns bowed. "Hail, your majesty, Harold, true king of England." Then they came to the table, trying to appear nonchalant as they jockeyed for a position close to the king. Falan, however, sat at the far end of the table.

Almost immediately servants appeared, carrying platters of roasted meat, trays of warm bread, bowls of steaming vegetables and jugs of beer, wine and mead, and the tent filled with the babble of conversations as the meal got under way. By now, we were used to eating with our hands, but I felt self-conscious in front of the king and tried to mimic the others, using the knives on hand to cut and skewer the food.

Throughout the meal, the Thegns and Harold congratulated us on our victory, and made us tell and retell events that we would have rather forgotten. I finally diverted them by asking the Thegns to tell of their victory and soon we were hearing graphic tales of more events that we would have preferred to forget. It had been bad enough watching the battle from a distance, but now we were seeing the slaughter through the eyes of the soldiers, with the Thegns leaving few details unspoken.

After the plates were cleared and more drinks were brought in, Harold raised his ostentatious silver chalice, while the Thengs raised their less impressive cups. "A toast, to our young friends, and saviours."

The Thegns jumped to their feet, cups raised,

cheering. Harold held up a hand. "But first, we establish their provenance."

I looked at Mitch. "Provenance?"

"They want to see if we're who we say we are."

"But we haven't said we're anybody."

"We know of their deeds," Harold said, speaking to the Thegns. "But you yourselves fought a larger hoard and returned victorious. Brave deeds and courage alone mean little in this regard, or you and your soldiers would all be knights. What matters is the cloak."

The table fell silent as the tent flap opened and Reinhart, accompanied by Blekwulf, Hoban and Gerwald, entered. Following, but keeping his distance, was Aelric, flanked by two soldiers. He looked nervous but determined, bowing to the king, and nodding to me and Mitch. Then another man entered, the old man we had seen with Falan just before the battle, still wearing his grey robe. In his hands, neatly folded and resting on a silver tray, he carried our cloak.

The Thegns looked at him and the cloak, murmuring excitedly amongst themselves.

Harold stood. All the Thegns jumped to their feet. Seeing we were the only ones still sitting, Mitch and I stood up as well. "Silence," Harold said. "This is a most grave matter, and its outcome may determine our fates." He swept a hand, indicating the old man. "Lubbik, Druid chief, seer, knower." He turned to the Thegns. "You thought the Druids long dead, a mere legend, perhaps, but they live on, a select few, guarding the Talisman for such a day as this. Lubbik, loyal friend and willing subject of the true king of England, is the cloak you hold the key to the Talisman?"

Lubbik nodded. "It is, your majesty."

The Thegns thumped the table and cheered. Harold

held up a hand to silence them. "And how did it come to you?"

"I received it from Lord Falan."

At this, Falan stood beside the Druid, facing the king.

"And how did the cloak come into your possession, Lord Falan?" Harold asked.

Without hesitation or embarrassment, Falan turned to Reinhart. "I took it from Huscarl Reinhart."

The murmuring of the Thegns grew louder. Harold ignored it and spoke over them. "Huscarl Reinhart, loyal friend, tell us, how did the cloak come to you?"

Reinhart's jaw tightened. He raised a hand, his finger pointing. "I took it from them."

The buzz of excited voices grew louder, some Thegns thumped the table. Harold waited until silence returned. Then he nodded to the soldiers escorting Aelric and they pushed him forward.

"Is this true?" Harold asked.

Aelric nodded. "I was with them. When the levy was recalled, Huscarl Reinhart saw their cloak, and he took it from them."

I looked at Harold. "See, it is ours. Can we have it back now?"

Harold chuckled and reached for his chalice, holding it out toward Reinhart. "You did a great service, for your king and kingdom, keeping the cloak safe for Lord Falan to bring to our noble Druid friend. He tipped his chalice in the direction of the old man. Falan beamed; the old man diverted his eyes.

The Thegns raised their cups, either in imitation of the king or in preparation for a toast. Then Harold called for silence.

"Lubbik has authenticated the cloak, true enough,"

he said. "But what of these young men? Brave warriors, of which we have no shortage, or the knights of legend? Speak on, my young friend, tell us how you know them."

I shuffled uncomfortably, feeling as if we were on trial. Aelric, also looking like he'd rather be any place else but there, cleared his throat. "They came to my cottage, in strange garments, carrying shields. They had the cloak with them."

"And what made you think they were not of this world?"

"They … they matched the stories, passed down through our family, about the warriors of old, who would one day return. And when they came into my house, they knew of a secret design, carved into a table, without having seen it. A design the one called Mitch says he himself carved hundreds of years ago."

"And can you reveal what that design looked like?"

Aelric looked confused and frightened. I caught his eye and, remembering Malcolm's words—to simply tell the truth—nodded to him.

"I … it is not something I could easily describe."

"Will you draw it for us, then?"

Aelric looked confused. "But—"

"Here and now," Harold said.

A servant appeared with a piece of parchment and a stick of charcoal. He gave them to Aelric, who then scratched on the parchment with the stick while Harold and the Thegns watched in silence. Even Reinhart's men stared at Aelric in wonder, while Reinhart himself continued to glare at Lubbik and the cloak. Only Harold and Falan seemed calm and not at all in suspense. It was, I thought, a set-up, a performance for the benefit of the Thegns.

Then Aelric put down the charcoal.

"Lord Falan," Harold said. "Show us what he has drawn."

With a flourish, Falan took the parchment and held it above is head. The stark black drawing was easy to see, even in the dim torch light. Aelric's rendering, however, didn't look as much like the outline of an airplane as it did an ornate cross. He even drew the knot in the wood, representing it as a black circle in the centre of the cross.

The tent erupted in cheers as the Thegns shouted and banged the table with their fists. Harold raised his arms and waited for silence. "This is a momentous event. It means the legends are indeed true. The knights have returned to sit here among us as flesh and blood. They are the Guardians of the Talisman, and they have brought their cloak to me, which means God has recognized me as the true king of England. It means," he raised his chalice high, its ornate inlays twinkling in the torchlight, "we cannot lose."

The Thegns let out a cheer and downed their cups. More drink was passed around and mugs of ale were handed to Reinhart and his men. Gerwald, Blekwulf and Hoban drank with gusto, but Reinhart drank grimly, glaring at me and Mitch as he did.

The Thegns crowded around Falan and Reinhart, thumping their backs, cheering them, raising shouts for victory. They toasted us repeatedly, shouting and cheering as they did. Amid the pandemonium, Harold spoke to us, quietly, a sly smile on his lips. "You have performed a great service, turning back the Viking raiders and bringing the cloak. You will, therefore, be kept close. For your own safety."

He paused to raise his glass as more toasts were

given.

"The threat has been dealt with; the season of war comes to an end. In two weeks, with the army rested and celebrations over, we will march south, releasing the levy men as we go. But you, my enigmatic friends, will remain with me. During the winter, you will go with Lord Falan and Lubbik to retrieve the Talisman. When William strikes in the spring, the Talisman, the cloak, and you, will be with me as I ride into battle. All my soldiers, and William himself, will know this. They will know I am the true King of England, and that no army can stand against me. So, you see, you must stay with me, as my guests."

I wondered if this was what Malcolm was afraid of. It sounded like a risky plan, like something someone who thought they couldn't lose would do.

"Thank you for your kindness," I said, hoping I didn't sound insincere, "but, as you said, we are the Guardians of the Talisman, and the cloak is ours. It should be with us, and the Talisman should remain where it is."

Harold smiled and shook his head, then looked to the Thegns and soldiers, who continued to cheer and toast. He raised his chalice and spoke quietly, while facing his guests, his words for our ears only.

"The cloak is made for a king, not commoners. You will have it when you retrieve the Talisman, and you will see it one last time on your final day, when you ride with me into battle where, I suspect, you will die bravely."

Chapter 33

Mitch

"Here we are again," I said. "Honoured guests."

"Otherwise known as prisoners," Charlie added.

We were in one of the Royal tents, sitting on our bed, which was just a cushion on a crude wooden frame. It was, however, filled with feathers instead of straw, and was a lot more comfortable than sleeping on the ground. Still, we would have rather been back in Malcolm's camp.

We didn't have anyone standing guard over us, but that didn't matter because Harold's soldiers were everywhere, and they watched us anytime we left the tent. The one good thing about our captivity was that we could at least see Aelric. He and the rest of the Sussex levy were still camping near the royal tents, and their camp did not seem to be off limits. We had seen him the day before, as we tested the boundaries of our captivity, and he had explained how the king's men had come to interrogate him about our visit. At first, they had grilled him about the family legends, which he knew little about, but once they found out about the carving in the table, they concentrated on that, and encouraged Aelric to draw a picture of it for them, that they could bring to Harold.

"So, it was all planned in advance," I said.

"They wanted to make sure everyone believed in

you," Aelric said, who seemed less suspicious of Harold's motives than we were. Harold was his king, and he wasn't going to think ill of him, but then Harold wasn't keeping him prisoner.

Aelric had been afraid that we would be angry at him for the part he had been forced to play, but we assured him he had done nothing wrong.

"All you did was tell the truth," I said.

"Besides," Charlie added, "we're closer to our cloak now."

And on this, our third morning of captivity, we decided to try to locate it.

Since we were not merely guests, like the Sussex levy, but royal guests of King Harold himself, our presence near the king's tents caused no alarm. The soldiers watched us, but with no single soldier assigned to be our guard—and with the drinking and carrying on with the York women occupying most of them— they took little notice.

When no one was looking, we stole between two tents, out of sight of the main camp, and squirmed beneath the walls to get a look at what was inside each of them., which was nothing of interest to us. Then we sneaked behind some others and looked in them. After several nerve wracking forays, without a glimpse of our cloak, we came to one of the larger tents in the tight cluster where Harold and his inner circle stayed.

Here, we would draw attention, so we waited until all the soldiers were occupied, then moved as quickly as we could—without looking panicked—to one of the tents near Harold's. Crouching in the shadows, we listened for cries of alarm, but none of the soldiers challenged us. I bent down and lifted the tent wall an inch and heard voices.

"There's someone in there," I whispered, easing the tent wall down.

Charlie nodded, and we waited. It seemed like hours, and every second we were sure someone was going to find us, but then the voices stopped, and we heard retreating footsteps and the rustle of the tent flap. I waited a few minutes, listening to make sure there was no one still in the tent, then quietly lifted the wall a few inches and peered under. When my eyes adjusted to the gloom, I gasped.

"What?" Charlie asked, squirming down close to me.

"It's here," I whispered.

He poked his head under, and we both stared in amazement. On a table, still folded and resting on the silver tray, was our cloak, no more than ten feet away.

"Let's get it!" Charlie said.

I put a hand on his back to keep him down and pointed to the far side of the room where, nearly hidden in the shadow, was Lubbik, reclining on a cushion. We froze, and waited, but he didn't sound an alarm. In fact, it seemed as if he hadn't seen us.

"I think he's asleep," I whispered.

"Do you think we can get it without waking him?" Charlie asked.

I nodded. "But I don't think we can get out of the camp with it."

"Shouldn't we try at least?"

Then we heard footsteps approaching. Lubbik sat up suddenly and looked toward the entrance, and Charlie and I took the opportunity to ease our heads out of the tent.

"Close one," Charlie said.

From inside the tent, we heard Falan's voice.

"I left you here to guard the cloak," he snapped, "and not ten minutes later I find you asleep. I should have you executed."

"I wasn't asleep, Lord Falan, I am vigilant. Always."

"Vigilant, yes, and a poor liar."

We crept silently away from the tent. When we thought we had gone far enough, we got up and walked, but we didn't get far.

"You there! Where do you think you're going?"

It was one of Harold's guards, and he didn't look happy.

"We're just walking," I said, hoping he would let us carry on.

But the pretence of us being guests was suddenly shattered when the guard called for soldiers to escort us back to our tent. They ushered us inside and ordered us to stay. Soon after, they brought food and drink, and left two soldiers outside to stand guard.

And so, we did the only thing we could do. We ate and, when evening came, we slept. We knew where the cloak was, we knew we would be traveling south soon, and we knew, somehow, we would get to see Malcolm. All we had to do was wait.

But we were awakened early, in the grey dawn, by a commotion in the camp. It wasn't raucous like the continual celebrations, or panicked like another attack, it was more random and chaotic. Men shouted, horses whinnied, and the tramping of footsteps—sometimes running, sometimes marching—sounded outside our tent. We pulled the flap open an inch and peered out. Men—soldiers and levy men alike—were busy deconstructing the camp.

There were no soldiers guarding our tent, and one of Harold's Huscarls strode about, his hand on the hilt of his sword, shouting orders. "Pack it up. Bring as much food as you can find. You levy men, pack your gear and return to your company. You will march with them. Step lively, we leave within the hour."

"Something's happened."

"Something big."

Another Huscarl left Harold's tent at a run. He stopped in front of Falan's tent, throwing the flap aside. It was too far away to hear more than an indistinct shout, but Falan and Lubbik stepped outside and, after conferring with the Huscarl, set off for Harold's tent.

"This is our chance," I said. "Everyone's too busy to notice us."

Then the Huscarl came toward our tent at a run, shouting to the soldiers around him. "Harold wants the Guardians. Bring them, now."

"We need to move," Charlie said.

We rushed to the back of the tent and scrambled under the wall. Moments later we heard shouts. "They've gone. Find them!" We scurried away, keeping close to the backs of the tents. When we reached the tent where our cloak was, we pulled up the wall and squirmed under.

"Do you think they saw us?" Charlie asked, as we sat on the ground, panting.

"They'd be here by now if they did," I said. "Quick, get the cloak."

But before we could move, we heard voices and approaching footsteps. Charlie dove for the wall but I grabbed him. "No. It's too dangerous out there. This way."

We darted to the other side of the tent and pulled Lubbik's mattress on top of us, laying as flat and still

168

as possible. I prayed that, whoever was coming, they would be too busy to notice the lumpy mattress, and that I could keep from sneezing.

The light in the tent went from dark to grey as the flaps were pulled aside and two people came in. I could only see their feet, but I recognized Falan's fancy shoes and the dirty fringe of Lubbik's robe.

"Pack it securely," Falan ordered. "And bring only what is necessary. Speed is of the essence."

"Lord Falan," Lubbik said. "This wasn't the plan. I … do you think this wise?"

"Listen," Falan hissed. "We leave with the king's blessing, our way to the Talisman is clear, that is proof of God's intervention. By His grace, we have the Guardians and the cloak. That proves He favours our mission."

"I never agreed to this. William was supposed to wait until spring, so we could spend the winter in negotiations. This was supposed to be a peaceful solution, a way to make Harold back down. If we take the Talisman to William now—"

The sound of a sword leaving its scabbard was followed by a whack and a thud as Lubbik fell to the ground. "You fool! There are spies everywhere. Watch your tongue or next time you will feel the sharp edge of my blade."

"But Lord Falan," Lubbik said, his voice pleading. "The Talisman was never meant to be used to barter with. If we continue on this path, I sense terrible things will happen."

"You fool even yourself," Falan said. "It was always going to come to this. Don't feign sentiment with me now; you're in as deep as I am."

"I … I no longer wish to be part of this."

"Your naivety amazes even me," Falan said. "I have the Guardians and the cloak, and no further use for you. Slitting your cowardly throat right now will be to my advantage. It will rid me of the burden of you and assure your silence. How do you like that plan?"

Falan sheathed his sword. Then I heard him pull his dagger.

"No, Lord Falan," Lubbik said, his voice shaking. "You heard the soldiers, the Guardians have escaped. You still need me. I am able to open the temple."

Falan stepped closer to him. "The Guardians will be found. They cannot be far."

"But if they escape, I am the only one who can help you."

I heard a grunt and saw Lubbik rise to his feet and figured Falan had pulled him up by the collar of his robe because there was more grunting and shuffling.

"Can you really open the temple?" Falan said. "And do not lie to me."

"I can," Lubbik said. "It should be the Guardians, that is how it is supposed to be, but I am able."

"Then you can thank whatever gods you pray to for saving your miserable life."

He must have pushed Lubbik because I heard him grunt again and then he crashed into the table and fell flat on the ground. The table lay on its side with the silver tray next to it, and next to that was our cloak.

"Bring the cloak" Falan said. "Leave the tray and everything else. We leave immediately."

Lubbik climbed to his feet. His hands picked up our cloak. Falan's feet retreated and Lubbik's followed.

We crawled out from under the mattress and went to the doorway, peeking through the narrow opening. Lubbik and Falan were heading to Harold's tent, and

Lubbik had our cloak.

"What do you think is going on?" Charlie asked.

"I don't know, but it must be big. They've changed their plans. They're going for the Talisman now."

"And we'll be going with them if they catch us."

Then we heard more shouting.

"We are finished here," a soldier yelled. "Take those tents down."

"Go," I said.

The soldiers were quick and well-practiced. Even as we slipped under the back wall, I felt the tent shudder and deflate as the main supports were pulled down. We ran toward Harold's tent, stopping to duck behind a cart piled high with supplies.

"We need to warn Harold," Charlie said.

"He'll never believe us," I said. "And then he'll never let us out of his sight."

"Then we need to get to Malcolm."

We peered around the edge of the cart. Across the camp, a band of soldiers poked at fallen tents and rifled through the carts.

"They're looking for us, we'll never get out of here."

Then a group of men, some with swords at their sides, others with shields slung on their backs, approached us.

"I think they're coming for the cart," Charlie said. "We've got to find another place to hide. Come on."

As the group drew near, I noticed that one of them was carrying an axe. I put a hand on Charlie's arm to keep him from running. "No, wait. That's Aelric. And men from the Sussex levy. They must be coming to take the cart back to their camp. Our camp."

We stayed hidden until the group was nearly upon us, then we stood up.

"Mitch, Charlie," Aelric said. "Why are you here? I thought—"

"We need to get back to the company," Charlie said.

"If you're going that way," I said, "we'll help you with the cart."

"Well, yes, we are, and you may certainly help us, but aren't you traveling with King Harold?"

"No," Charlie said. "We're being sent back to the levy."

Aelric looked confused. I leaned close. "Listen, Aelric," I said, "it wouldn't be good for us to be seen. It might slow us down and, we're, you know, sort of celebrities now—"

"Celebrities?"

"Well known," I continued. "People will want to stop us and talk to us. It will impede our progress and we need to get there quickly. Harold, I mean, King Harold, wants us to hurry. And I suspect Reinhart has not softened during our absence."

At the mention of Reinhart, the men looked alarmed.

"But how," Aelric asked.

"Can we borrow some shields?" I asked.

"And hats?" Charlie added.

With the shields slung on our backs and hats pulled tight over our heads, we looked like any of the other levy men and drew no attention as we pushed the heavy cart through the camp, back to Reinhart's company.

As we approached, we saw Malcolm, calmly packing up his cooking equipment.

"Thanks, Aelric," I said, taking off the shield.

"Yeah," Charlie said, handing his hat back to its owner. "We've got to see Malcolm."

"But Reinhart will expect you to report to him."

"We will, just not yet."

We left the bewildered men and the slightly annoyed Aelric and raced to Malcolm's camp. He looked up as we approached. For all his calm demeanour, his face was grave.

"Malcolm," I said, running up to him. "Falan and Lubbik are leaving to get the Talisman. And they have our cloak with them."

Malcolm nodded. "And what of Harold? Does he know?"

I thought for a moment. "He believes they are bringing it to him. But they're going to double-cross him. They're going to take it to William. But he's still in Normandy."

Malcolm shook his head. "William has landed on the south coast, and Harold is hurrying to meet him."

"That's the battle he was talking about," Charlie said, his face white. "The one where he wants us and our cloak with him, so he can win, and we can get slaughtered."

"It's coming sooner than he thought," I said. "That's why he wanted us. We're supposed to get the Talisman for him. But if we're gone, it must be safe. You said only the Guardians, with the cloak, can access it. Was Lubbik lying about being able to get it, just to save his skin?"

Malcolm looked at the ground and shook his head. "It is worse than I thought. Desperate times are tempting desperate men to take desperate measures. Lubbik, no doubt, told Falan that he could access the Talisman to save his life, but that does not mean it is not true. He knows, as I do, the ancient ways and, in possession of the cloak, he could open the door, but it would be folly. The Talisman would know, and

173

nothing good could come of it." Then he looked at me. "How was Harold when you met him? What sort of man did you take him to be?"

I thought for a moment. "He seems drunk with power."

"He believes he is invincible," Charlie said. "He gave our cloak to Lubbik, and he held us captive. And now he's after us."

"Then we must leave immediately," Malcolm said. "Get your shields. I will get horses. We must stop Falan and Lubbik. And keep you out of Harold's hands."

"You're running away?" We turned to see Aelric standing behind us. "You've just gained the king's favour. Reinhart can't touch you now, and you're going to desert? That's madness. That's treason. Reinhart will kill you, you know that."

"We don't want to," Charlie said. "We have to."

"We took an oath," Aelric said, his voice rising, "to serve the king. You can't break that. I won't let you, not after all we've been through."

Malcolm stepped near to Aelric. "There are other ways, aside from war, to serve."

With that, Malcolm strode away.

"Listen, Aelric," I said. "You've got to go before someone sees you talking to us."

"We have to go," Charlie said, strapping his shield on. "We have to get our cloak back."

"And save the Talisman," I said.

We heard horse hoofs approaching. Malcolm, riding one horse and leading two others, galloped toward us. We turned to go meet him, but Aelric gripped us each by an arm. "Will I see you again?"

"I don't know," Charlie said, shaking his head.

"God go with you," Aelric said, releasing us.

I looked at Aelric. "We're all doing what we have to do," I said, "but we follow different paths. Stay true and, with luck, we will meet again."

Chapter 34

Charlie

The horses Malcolm brought were saddled and loaded with packs. "Quickly," he said. "These will soon be missed."

We each jumped on a horse and, with Malcolm leading the way, galloped through the camp.

"Hey!"

"What the—"

The startled soldiers cried out as we clatter among them, avoiding wagons and columns of men.

"Stop them," someone cried.

We pressed on, clinging as tight as I could to the reins, my jaw clenched, my knees digging into the flanks of my horse. The main entrance came in sight, blocked by a column of soldiers. We veered away, toward open land. Then another group of men came in from the side, running to cut us off. Malcolm kept on, heading straight toward them. As his horse bore down on them, they panicked and scrambled. Malcolm's horse shot through the gap, and me and Mitch followed. Behind us came shouts, but fortunately no arrows. We galloped on, my bones jarring as we raced over the open fields, away from the camp.

We travelled down the roads we had come in on, galloping for what seemed like hours, until Malcolm halted the horses to let them rest and graze. The road stretched before us, winding over hills and disappearing into valleys. There were few travellers visible, and Falan and Lubbik were not among them.

"I don't see them," Mitch said. "Did they go a different way?"

"There is no different way," Malcolm said. "Not here. They will be ahead of us. Far ahead. They have the best horses, and an urgency greater even than that of the king himself."

We mounted and rode on, not at a full gallop, but more of a fast trot that bounced me painfully in the saddle.

"We will make better time in the long run this way," Malcolm said, when he noticed my discomfort. "A horse can only gallop for so long. This is a comfortable pace for them, though not so comfortable for the riders. Don't worry, you will get used to it."

We trotted on, passing travellers now and again, keeping an eye on the road ahead. We rode, rested, and rode again, over and over, until the evening drew in. When it became too dangerous for the horses, we left the road and camped behind a stand of trees.

After tethering the horses, Malcolm showed us how to rub them down. Then he left us and disappeared into the woodland.

"Where do you suppose he keeps going off to?" I asked.

Mitch rubbed the brush we had found in the saddle bags over his horse's flank. "I don't know, but I hope he's gathering more rabbits. I'm starving."

But Malcolm returned only with a handful of herbs and unwelcome news.

"We are being followed," he said. "I spied a

campfire some distance away.

My heart sank. "Is it Reinhart?"

"I fear it is, he and his trusted men, Hoban, Gerwald and Blekwulf."

I shuddered at the memory of the deserting levy man's execution. "He won't ... I mean, Harold will want us back."

"We can only hope," Malcolm said. "But for now, speed and stealth are our friends."

We didn't dare light a fire, so dinner was cheese and some cold meat we found in the saddle bags. Then we laid on the ground near the horses. I shivered in the cold under my thin blanket, my muscles aching, my backside throbbing.

Malcolm, who had been sitting on his own, came to us as I was finally falling asleep.

"Here," he said, holding something out to me.

"What is it?"

He handed me a cup containing a thick, foul-smelling paste. "It is a balm, or a potion; it will sooth your pains."

Both me and Mitch scooped the paste from the cup and rubbed it onto our sore muscles. Then I fell asleep, while Malcolm stood, staring into the night sky.

Malcolm woke us before dawn, when the eastern sky was just beginning to glow. "Our adversaries will be on the move soon. We must go now."

We saddled the horses and rode on, eating a breakfast of dry bread and cheese as we plodded along. When the sky brightened enough to see, we urged the horses into a trot, and I was pleasantly surprised to find that the pain of the day before was gone. Either that, or I was simply too tired to feel it.

Before the sun was high, we turned off the road to

Lincoln onto a road heading south.

"How do you know they went this way," I asked.

"They didn't," Malcolm answered. "I know Falan's destination; I do not need to follow his route. This way is shorter, but more rugged; they will make better time on the flatter roads to the east."

"Then why don't we go that way?"

Malcolm looked bemused. "Because you are young and strong and will make better time in the mountains, and we will have a better chance of evading our pursuers in the more rugged land."

So we turned off the main road and headed into the forest, toward the mountains.

The trees became thicker as we followed the narrow road up steep inclines and through dense valleys. The road was in bad condition, and we often found ourselves picking our way through the forest. By nightfall, we had not seen another human being.

Dark came early in the forest and forced us to stop sooner than we would have liked. After tending the horses, Malcolm led us up a nearby peak where, through a break in the trees, we saw the distant glow of a campfire.

"Our pursuers are tenacious, indeed," Malcolm said. "But we should expect nothing less. Harold is determined to capture you and bring you back."

"And Reinhart?"

"He is simply determined to capture you. Whether to follow the king's wishes or his own I cannot say. It is best we do not find out."

We ate another cold meal, spent another short night shivering under our blankets and, in the grey dawn, were back on the road.

"We must press our advantage while we can,"

Malcolm told us as we grumbled over our meagre breakfast. "In this wilderness, Reinhart cannot afford to push his horses beyond their limits. Here, we can ride as fast as he can. Once we get to the flat land, he will ride his horses to death, and steal others from the farmers."

That night, when we climbed to view the trail behind us, Reinhart's campfire was closer.

"They will be upon us tomorrow," Malcolm said. "Unless we can fool them."

"Can we?"

"We must."

◆

Well before dawn we started, picking our way through the dark along the rocky path, leading our horses by the reins. As soon as it became light enough to see, we mounted and rode at a fast trot and, by sunup, we had left the hills behind. We stopped by a stream to rest, letting the horses graze and drink their fill. We ate what little food we had, then set out again. As the sun rose high, we began to see other people, walking or driving carts, and an hour or so later, we saw what appeared to be a small village protected by an earthen wall and flanked by a river. The road, now broad and rutted by cart wheels, led across a bridge that spanned the river and entered the village through a gap in the wall.

After the clear air of the hills, the stench of the village was shocking, but being around people was a comfort and I soon grew accustomed to the smell. The village consisted of a few rows of stone cottages, hundreds of chickens and pigs running free, and lots of mud. An open area in the centre served as a marketplace where a few barrows were parked containing vegetables, animal carcasses and a lot of stuff I couldn't identify. Men and women haggled and traded and nearby, outside a larger dwelling that appeared to be a public house, a group of men were drinking from wooden mugs.

We rode down the main street and through the marketplace, guiding our horses around the men, woman, chickens, and children. We rode without speaking to anyone, but Malcolm kept a careful watch on the men buying and selling. One in particular seemed to interest him, a tall man with black hair and an unruly beard. His clothes looked better made than most, but they were dusty and worn. A sword and dagger hung from the man's belt. Malcolm watched him until the man looked our way, then he nodded a greeting to the man, and we rode on.

In a short time, we passed through the village and headed down a straight, nearly flat road, bordered by hedgerows, grasslands, and distant forests. I expected Malcolm to break into a gallop, but instead he trotted, checking over his shoulder occasionally until the town was out of sight. Then he stopped.

"What are we doing?"

"Stopping for Lunch," Malcolm said. He dismounted, rubbed his back, and stretched. "I think we deserve a leisurely meal."

Me and Mitch looked at each other. We were famished and fatigued, yet it seemed a crazy idea; not only were we in a hurry, we also didn't have any food. We turned to Malcolm. "But Reinhart, and the Talisman," Mitch said.

"And our cloak," I said.

"Reinhart knows he is closing in on us. He is a

cunning hunter and will not want to take chances. He will not rush through the town, but will search it thoroughly, questioning, making sure no one is helping us, and probably taking as much food and drink as he and his men can wish."

Unlike us, I thought, though I said nothing. We had no money to buy food, or anything to barter with, so our lack of food wasn't Malcolm's fault, but we still needed to outrun Reinhart.

"So, we should keep going then, to increase our lead."

Malcolm led his horse into the grass to let it graze. We dismounted and followed.

"Our horses need rest. So do we. With luck, this is where we will lose Reinhart. And have a nice meal as well."

"But we have no food," Mitch said.

"Not yet," Malcolm said.

We tethered our horses, then sat in the grass a distance away, watching Malcolm build a fire. I burned with curiosity, wondering what he was up to, but he gave no clue and said nothing except to tell us to gather more wood and unburden the horses. We left the saddles on them, but took off the saddle bags and our shields, piling them in the tall grass near the horses, with our shields under the packs as Malcolm instructed.

Then we sat at the fire and drank the last of our water. It was barely enough to dull the sharp edge of my thirst, but it was good to sit on soft grass again instead of hard leather, and to not be running for our lives. Even so, I felt anxious, wondering what Malcolm was waiting for.

A few minutes later, Malcolm stood and looked

down the road. "Here comes our unlikely saviour."

We peered into the distance. A single man riding a horse was coming our way. It was the man we had seen in the market. "Who is it?" I asked.

"I don't know who he is," Malcolm said. "I only know what he is, a scalawag."

"A what?"

"A thief, a highwayman. I am hoping he will try to rob us. Sit down and look harmless. But be ready. We may need to subdue him in order to request his help. Many such men as he are ruthless."

Mitch leaned close to me. "He was big," he whispered.

"And armed," I reminded him.

Mitch nodded. "But no more than a Viking."

The man came toward us at a slow trot. When he was near, he stopped.

"Would you care for the company of a fellow traveller at your meal? I have meat and bread to share." Without waiting for an answer, the man dismounted and walked into the field, tethering his horse near ours.

Malcolm stood slowly, rubbing his back, and standing slightly stooped. "We would, kind sir. I and my grandsons have little to share, but we share it gladly." He turned to me and Mitch. "Fetch the rest of the food from the saddle bags." As he spoke, he pointed his index fingers at us and made a half circle with each. We both nodded and went toward the horses, behind the man who continued to face Malcolm.

We took the shields from where we had left them and crept up behind the man, me coming in on his left, and Mitch on his right. Even from a distance his smell stung my nostrils.

"I think, perhaps, you have much to share," the man said, his voice suddenly menacing. Then he drew his sword and pointed it at Malcolm. "Fine horses and tackle, and whatever supplies you have. It will do me much good, and it will soon be of no use to you and your grandsons."

Malcolm stepped back, cowering. "Please, sir, take what you will, but do not harm us"

The man spat. "And leave you to go to the guards? Perhaps I will kill you only, and tie your grandsons to stakes for the wolves to do my work."

Then Malcolm stood to his full height. "You threaten us, sir?"

The man stepped back, surprised. But he recovered and replied: "I do." Then he lunged for Malcolm.

Chapter 35

Mitch

The thief swung his sword at Malcolm, but Malcolm wasn't there. He had moved aside faster than the thief had anticipated, and now he hesitated, confused, and Charlie and I took the opportunity to rush him. He heard us coming and turned, lashing out with his sword but hitting my shield instead of my neck. The blow glanced off and Charlie smashed into him, driving him toward me. I held up my shield and we pinned him between us. Malcolm moved fast and came up behind him. In one swift movement he pulled the thief's knife from his belt and held it to his throat.

"Lay down your weapon."

The sword thudded to the ground. "Don't kill me."

"You beg for mercy when you show none."

"A jest," the man cried. "A jest. Take of mine what you will, but leave me my life."

We lowered our shields. Malcolm pulled him backward, and turned him around, still pointing the knife at his throat. I grabbed up the fallen sword and stood ready.

"I will spare your life," Malcolm said. "If you will do us a service."

"Anything," the man said, his voice rising in panic.

"Steal our horses."

The man blinked. "What did you say?"

"Steal our horses. Leave us the blankets and your provisions, but take our horses."

The man gaped at Malcolm for a few seconds. Then he smiled. "I know when something is too good to be true, and this is. What is the catch?"

"There are men after us. They will follow our horses, while we take to the river."

The man's smile faltered. "How many men."

"Four. And they are soldiers."

The man pondered for a moment. "A worthy challenge. Shall we shake on the deal?"

"I would sooner kiss an adder," Malcolm said. Then he looked to me and Charlie. "Go to his horse. Take what food is in his bags, then gather our packs. And stay clear until our horses, and this scoundrel, are out of sight."

After we had gathered everything, the man went back to the horses and tied their reins to a long rope. Then he mounted his own horse. "Surely you will not send me away unarmed."

Malcolm took the sword from me and handed it back to the thief. "The sword you may keep, but your knife may come in handy." He tucked the knife into his belt and stepped away. "You had best be quick. Our pursuers are not far behind."

The man trotted away, leading our horses in a line. He glanced nervously up the road, then headed south at a gallop.

Malcolm watched until the man, and our horses, crested a low rise and disappeared down the far side. "Quickly," he said. "To the forest."

We doused the fire, picked up our packs and followed him. "But I thought we were going by boat."

"When Reinhart catches that thief, as he surely will,

he will gladly tell them all he knows about us in trade for his life. Reinhart will look to the rivers, and we will be in the forest."

As we reached the trees, we looked back at the road. In the distance, four horsemen rode at a gallop. We moved further into the woods, out of sight.

"With luck," Malcolm said, "we can stop worrying about him for a while."

"Just a while?" Charlie asked. "I thought we lost him for good."

"As in our pursuit of Falan, Reinhart does not know our route, but he knows our destination. The closer we get to the Tor, the more danger we will be in. But for now, we are safe."

We followed Malcolm into the forest, who seemingly wandered at random.

"The Roman's built fine roads to move armies, but the ancient paths are still here. We can make good time on them, but we cannot tarry."

"Falan has horses," Charlie protested. "How are we supposed to catch them?"

"Falan also has Lubbik," Malcolm replied. "It is he I am counting on."

"Counting on how?" I asked.

"If what you say is true, his spirit is not in his mission. He is reluctant and will slow Falan down. Not a lot, but perhaps enough to keep him from getting to the tor before us."

The path, when Malcolm found it, was hard packed earth, winding through the undergrowth and weaving between the dense trees. It was only wide enough for us to travel single file, but we soon fell into the familiar rhythm of putting one foot in front of the other.

The trek through the forest was almost pleasant

compared to what we had been through. For now, the constant threat of violence was behind us, and the trees shaded us from the sun and kept us hidden. We shared out the bread and meat we had liberated from the thief and ate it as we walked. The thief had had no water, but we drank from streams and springs that Malcolm pointed out along the way.

As darkness descended, Malcolm built a fire and for the first time in days we ate a hot meal of roasted rabbit. In the morning, Malcolm showed us how to gather mushrooms and berries and we filled our packs with as much as we could find while Malcolm filled his herb sack and caught another rabbit or two.

The paths we followed took us over hills and into valleys where the way was smooth and straight. Occasionally we followed farm tracks or roads that passed through settlements or small villages. At these times, we quickened our pace, always mindful that, although we were making better time, both Falan and Reinhart had the advantage of horses and smoother roads. Then we would disappear back into the forest.

On our third day of walking, the forest thinned, and we entered an undulating land of tall grass and shrubs. The blue sky and sun of the morning gave way to dull clouds and drizzle by noon, and we walked on, getting damper and damper. In the late afternoon the sun reappeared, and we saw, in the distance, a ragged line of people—groups walking together, others riding horses or pushing carts—some heading north, others south.

"What are they doing?" I asked.

"That is the road to Cirencester," Malcolm said. "With luck, Falan and Lubbik or at least news of them, might be found there."

"Is that where we're going?" Charlie asked. I hoped we were, there might be food there. But Malcolm shook his head.

"As we are, the risk is too great. Reinhart will surely pick up his search for us there, and if Reinhart is in the city, he will certainly hear of us. We are not exactly inconspicuous."

I looked at Charlie and Malcolm, and then at myself. In addition to being an old man with a dagger in his belt, accompanied by the two of us carrying battered shields, we were dirtier and more dishevelled than an average traveller.

Charlie sighed. "Back to the forest, then?"

Malcolm didn't answer. In silence, he stared into the distance, where the road disappeared in the direction of the place he called Cirencester, seemingly deep in thought. "As we are," he said after a long pause, "we would surely be noticed. But as an old man traveling on his own, I might have a chance."

"What about us?"

"The city will be dangerous for you. We will need to split up and meet on the far side. In daylight, I would have you go around, but in the night you risk being taken by thieves."

"Give us the knife, then," Charlie said. "We can protect ourselves."

"I need the knife to trade for food, and thieves do not always come alone, nor do they announce their presence. You would be taken by surprise, and by a superior number. No, you will need to go through the city, but we must make ourselves as unobtrusive as we can."

We retraced our steps to a brook near the forest edge and washed vigorously in the frigid water. Then we scrubbed our clothing, removing as much dust and dirt as possible. Cleaned and dressed in our newly washed, though wet, clothes, we didn't look much different from anyone else on the road. Except for the obvious.

"Our shields," I said. "They'll give us away."

"Then I will take them," Malcolm said.

To make them as inconspicuous as possible, we laid them together and bound them in one of our blankets. Then we wrapped the other blankets—stuffed with the few supplies in our packs—around it to make it look like a large bundle. It was heavy, but not anything Malcolm couldn't handle, and when he put it on his back, he looked like any other traveller with a large pack. Our packs, however, were empty, which made them look strange. I put Charlie's pack in mine, but it still looked too light, so I added a few rocks to make it look more substantial.

When we finished, Malcolm put on his pack and looked us over. "If we go through the city separately," he said, nodding in approval, "we will be as anonymous as any other person on the road."

We headed back toward the road and, as we drew near, Malcolm told us to separate.

"Remain in sight," he said, "but do not appear to be together. By the time we reach the city, darkness will be falling. That will also help to cover us."

An hour later, as we approached the city, dusk was settling in.

"Move away from me now," Malcolm said. "Appear to be lone travellers. Walk straight through the city, do not stop, talk to no one, and hide near the side of the road when you get to the far side. I will join you there."

In the twilight, we saw, the city, enclosed by a

derelict wall with houses and fields spilling out into the surrounding area. We followed the traffic through the city gates, entering a claustrophobic confusion of shouts and jostling and horrific smells. I kept my eyes on Charlie's back. Ahead of him, I caught glimpses of Malcolm as he wove his way through the crowded street.

Solid rows of houses on either side of the street gave me a feeling of being trapped in a canyon, with a river of people funnelling through it. The crowds thinned as we came to an open area in the centre of the town. Here, people were heading out of the marketplace while we were going in and the stall holders were packing up for the evening.

Malcolm paused now and again, haggling with impatient stall holders, and talking with other travellers. Soon, Charlie and I made our way past him, and returned to the narrow, crowded street. Ahead of us, the city gate stood open. It was guarded, but the sentries were taking little notice of the people passing in and out. We were nearly there. Then I saw Charlie stumble as a hand came out of the crowd and grabbed him by the shoulder. I stopped, shocked, as Reinhart stepped into view. "Got you," he said.

Charlie struggled but I knew it was futile. The only good thing was, Reinhart was facing away from me. I was close to him, and he didn't know I was there. But then, I didn't know where Gerwald, Hoban and Blekwulf were.

Then Reinhart spun Charlie around and pulled him close. "Where's your brother," he shouted, his nose barely and inch from Charlie's. "Tell me now, or die where you stand."

Chapter 36

Charlie

Reinhart's big hand squeezed me around the throat and lifted me, kicking and gasping, as my feet left the cobbles.

"Tell me," he said again. "Give a nod and I'll let you go."

My vision began to blur, then go dark. The last thing I saw was Mitch, coming up from behind. He had his pack in his hand, holding it by the strap, swinging it in a long arc, aimed at Reinhart's head. Then everything went black.

When I woke, I was lying on the road, gasping for breath, with Mitch kneeling over me and Reinhart lying beside me.

"Wake up," Mitch yelled. He helped me to my feet. "Are you all right."

I gasped a few more times, then nodded. And then I saw Gerwald, Blekwulf and Hoban making their way through the crowd toward us.

"No," I said. "Run."

At that same instant, Reinhart's eyes opened, and he made a grab for us. "Stop them," he bellowed.

We dodged around people and livestock, heading for the city gate, ignoring the angry shouts that came our way. The commotion caught the attention of the guards, who stepped into the road, blocking our path, their swords held ready.

"This way," Mitch said.

We ducked down a side street barely wide enough for a cart, fighting our way through a throng of people that grew thicker and slower. We pushed through, shoving people aside, and soon saw the reason for the hold up. A cart, taking up the whole of the street, was making its way slowly between the buildings. Behind us we heard the shouts of Reinhart and his men. We edged nearer to the cart, bowling people over, but when we got to it, we found it wedged between two buildings.

"We can't get around it," I said.

"Crawl under."

We dropped to the cobbles and crawled forward, squirming under the cart, and coming out between the front wheels and the horses. The driver swung a stick at us. "What do you think you're doing?" We ducked and ran up the nearly deserted lane. The shouts grew distant and dim, but then I heard hoof beats coming our way.

We ran, but the horses drew nearer. There were more than four. Reinhard must have called on the guards to help. The sound of hooves clopping on stone was all around us now, echoing through the streets while their riders shouted to one another. The voice we heard most often and most clearly was Reinhart's. We came to a crossroads with lanes branching off in every direction but had no idea where they led to, and no idea which, if any, of them was not occupied by one or more of the horsemen. We stood in the open road, paralysed with indecision, listening to the sounds of shouting and galloping growing louder and nearer.

I turned in a circle, looking and listening, but no

direction seemed safe.

"What do we do now?" I asked.

Before Mitch could answer, I heard a voice calling from the shadows. "Mitch, Charlie, this way."

It was Malcolm. We ran after him as he led us through a narrow path between the houses. We squeezed through the opening, then froze, panting in the shadows, as the city guards rode by. Malcolm motioned to us, and we followed deeper into a labyrinth of pathways, courtyards, and narrow lanes until we came to a dead end.

Our pursuers, who were never far away, even as we had dodged through the maze, drew nearer.

"Over the wall," Malcolm said. "Quickly."

Mitch looked at the stone wall blocking Our path. "I can't get over that."

I ran to one of the houses clustered against the wall, scrambled onto the roof, then onto the roof of a taller house. "It's easy," I said. "Come on." From there, I grabbed the top of the wall and hoisted myself up.

Mitch and Malcolm followed. Soon the three of us were lying on top of the thick wall, looking into the darkness on the far side.

"There are houses built on the outside too," Malcolm said. "We can climb down. But keep silent. Reinhart will soon realize where we went. Remaining unobserved will be to our advantage."

We moved around the wall until we found a roof within jumping distance, then climbed down quickly and quietly. Away from the city lights, the night sky became visible, and the full moon illuminated our surroundings enough for us to move confidently and silently. Malcolm led us back into the forest, to a clearing, where we sat and rested.

Malcolm had traded the thief's knife for some food. We ate it in silence, then drank from a nearby spring.

"Are you feeling rested and refreshed?" Malcolm asked.

I exchanged a worried glance with Mitch. "Aren't we camping here for the night?"

Malcolm shook his head. "We have a momentary advantage. Falan is ahead of us, and Reinhart is close on our heels, but we can change that if we act."

"Falan is here?" I asked.

Mitch jumped to his feet. "With our cloak?"

Malcolm motioned for us to sit. "Falan was here, sometime after midday. He and Lubbik set off on the road to Bath a few hours ago. They will not have gone far before they had to stop for the night."

"Can't we catch them?" I asked. "Take them by surprise?"

"In the dark, everyone looks the same," Malcolm said. "Our time would be better spent taking the lead rather than waking every sleeping traveller we spot along the road. Reinhart will do that for us. He will come after us, but not until he is satisfied that we are not still in the city or hiding just outside the walls. They will turn the city upside down, and then send scouts out on every road leading from the city to look for us. Only after we are not found will he set out on the road to Bath. So now is our opportunity to outdistance him. He will not suspect it, he will assume we are too weary, and wary of the night, to travel far."

"Aren't we?" Mitch asked.

"Only if you want to prove him right."

Mitch sighed. I slung my shield over my shoulder. "Well, I don't," I said, rising to my feet.

Reluctantly, Mitch stood next to me. Malcolm

smiled. "Do not look so downhearted. We are in my country. I know this land. I know the people. We will walk the ancient paths where there is little chance of encountering foes, and some chance that we may find assistance along the way."

Malcolm turned and walked away, into the dense forest where only occasional shafts of moonlight lit the way. I took a deep breath, glanced up at the full moon, and followed him into darkness.

Chapter 37

Mitch

We made slow but steady progress. Malcolm, guided by his familiarity of the land and the sporadic light of the moon, led us deeper and deeper into the forest. Hours later, when the night was at its coldest and the moon was setting, Malcolm led us off the path where, in the pitch dark, with the chill seeping into my bones, he allowed us to sit while he made a small fire. After admonishing us to not stray away from it, no matter what happened, he disappeared into the forest.

When he returned, he had a stout stick, split at one end with lengths of tree bark and vines wound around it. He held it to the small flame of our fire until the woven materials caught.

"A torch?" Charlie asked.

Malcolm nodded. "To help us see, and to help others see us."

"Others?" I asked. But he ignored me.

"Douse the fire and follow," he said in a whisper.

The torch lasted only a few minutes, but it was enough to allow us to get out of the forest. As the torch began to sputter out, the stars appeared overhead, signifying that we were now in open land. Malcolm stopped, holding the smouldering torch, its dying embers still visible in the dark night. Then a voice called from the blackness. "Stop and be recognized, or feel the tip of my arrow."

Malcolm held the dying torch in front of his face. "It is I," he said.

Then figures appeared from the darkness, and torches came alight. Two men in robes with white beards stepped forward, followed by younger men wearing long smocks and leather trousers, and carrying bows and arrows. "Brother," the men in the robes said as they hugged Malcolm, one after the other. "What brings you here? It cannot be good news."

"Indeed, it is not," Malcolm said. "But there will be time for talk later. Right now, I need food and rest, for myself and my companions."

Charlie and I stepped forward, holding our shields protectively in front of us. The younger men raised their bows. "Saxon warriors," the nearest one said.

"Stay your weapons," Malcolm said. "They are indeed warriors, but no Saxons." He turned to us. "Mitch, Charlie. Put down your shields. You are among friends. Step into the light that they may see you."

I slung my shield over my shoulder and, with an uncertain glance at Charlie, stepped forward. The men in the robes looked at us, their eyes wide.

One of them held his torch uncomfortably close to my face, gazed into my eyes, and ruffled my hair. Then did the same to Charlie. "The prophecy has come true," he said.

"Is it the two?" the other asked.

"Yes," Malcolm said. "And we need rest, then food, and then I must ask your assistance."

"Whatever you wish, we will provide," the old man said. "Come this way."

After a short walk, we entered what appeared to be a small settlement. Fires were lit and more torches appeared, providing dim illumination to a ring of circular stone huts topped with cones of thatch. From the doorways, women and children eyed us with a mixture of suspicion and curiosity.

The old man stopped in front of a hut. "You may rest in here."

Malcolm nodded his thanks and stepped through the curtained doorway. Charlie and I prepared to follow, but the old man laid a hand on my shoulder. "You will be safe here." I looked at the old man's eyes and believed him, deeply and truly. It was a strange feeling, safe. I had been in danger for so long I had forgotten what it felt like, and it felt like a weight lifting from my shoulders. Suddenly, I was very tired.

"Thank you," I said.

Inside, it was inky black. I felt my way to a straw mattress and scrabbled around for a blanket. Then I laid my shield aside, fell next to Charlie, and was asleep as soon as my head hit the straw.

◆

When I awoke from the most comfortable and untroubled sleep I'd had since we arrived, dim light filtered through the slats covering the window openings and around the edges of the blanket serving as a door. Sounds from outside confirmed that people were up and busy, though the quality of the light indicated it was still early morning.

Charlie and I emerged to find a group of men loading a narrow cart with straw and hitching it to two horses. Malcolm was with them, talking to the old man. When they saw us, the old man turned and smiled. "Ah, the warriors awake." Charlie and I nodded, not knowing what to say.

"They are modest," Malcolm said, "but don't let their mild manner deceive you, they saved Harold's army from a surprise attack by the Vikings, and defeated them, though they were outmatched." Which wasn't the same as being outnumbered, I thought.

The old man gave a small bow. "Your modesty suits you. I am honoured to meet you, and I thank you for the privilege of helping you on your way." He swept his hand toward the group preparing the cart. "These men will take you as near as they can to the Sacred Tor. From there, it will be up to you. I will pray to the gods for a safe journey and successful outcome."

I looked at the cart. Its narrowness made it appear unstable and there seemed to be little enough room for the straw, let alone the three of us. "Are we to ride in that?" I asked.

"Yes," the old man said. "More humble than you are used to, but it will get you where you need to go."

Dawn was just breaking, and the day was cloudy and cool. When the cart was ready, we fetched our shields, and the blankets, and climbed awkwardly into the cart. I saw that, in addition to straw, the cart was also loaded with food and water. Malcolm climbed in after us and we sat, with Malcolm at one end, and me and Charlie at the other, wrapped in our blankets.

The driver climbed into the rickety seat, flicked the reins and the cart lurched forward, making a wide circle around the enclosure and then onto the narrow path we had come in on the night before. The path was so narrow that half a dozen men had to guide the cart, holding on to the back and front, so it wouldn't slip sideways into the brush. When we got to the main path, we saw the reason for its curious construction. The path we had been on looked like a narrow groove in the forest. The cut was so deep into the ground that the steep sides were higher than the cart, higher than the horses, even. The forest above us, right up to the edge of the cut, was thick with trees and shrubs. As soon as we were settled on the main path, most of the men returned to the village, leaving only two who walked silently behind the cart. Each of them carrying a bow and a quiver of arrows.

The path was beaten hard by years of travel, it's surface firm and smooth and soon, lulled by the gentle rocking of the cart, I fell back asleep.

I woke when the day was brighter, but still overcast, and ate a meal of cheese and bread. The men and the driver ate, too, but the food was passed to them and eaten as they walked.

As the day wore on, the men took turns driving the cart and walking. In this way, they were able to keep a steady pace and by late afternoon the trees began to thin and soon we were traveling over low hills covered in brush. When the light began to fade, we entered a broad meadow of tall grass, and the land became flat. Free from the forest and traveling on level ground, we could see for miles. Ahead of us, the land was speckled with pools of water and far in the distance, noticeable because it was the only feature on the flat landscape, was a hill, standing lonely above the watery meadows surrounding it.

"What's that?" Charlie asked, pointing into the distance.

"That," Malcolm said, although he had not turned to look, "is the Sacred Tor."

"Is that where Falan is going," I asked.

"Yes. And if the gods are willing, we will get there

ahead of him."

"And do what?"

"Stop him from stealing the Talisman."

"And get our cloak back," Charlie said.

Malcolm smiled. "Yes. And if we fail in our mission, that will be the most important part. The Land will suffer greatly if the Talisman finds its way to William. But a larger tragedy will come if you are not returned home safely."

I had a dozen questions to ask, but I saw Malcolm turn away, looking deep in thought and troubled, so I kept quiet.

The cart stopped in a grassy meadow, just on the edge of the wetlands. It was nearly dark, so we made camp, ate, and laid down by a warming fire while the men from the village kept watch.

"Tomorrow, we go to the Tor," Malcolm said, "so get what food and sleep you can. I fear more troubles await us."

With that, he fell asleep, But I laid awake for a long time, looking into the black sky, listening to the sounds of night, and wondering what waited for us on the imposing, distant hill.

Chapter 38

Charlie

In the morning we ate, packed food and water, and bid our companions goodbye. The men drove the cart back to their village and, once they left us, I thought I had never felt so alone in my life. All around, as far as I could see, there was nothing and no one, just an endless expanse of flat land, shrouded in places by patches of mist, with the Tor, now an object of some foreboding, on the horizon.

Malcolm stood, facing the Tor. "From here on," he said, "the land is treacherous. Follow my footsteps carefully. If you stray, you may be swallowed by the swamp."

I took an involuntary step backward. Malcolm smiled. "Do not be afraid. I know the path well, and it is safe enough, as long as you keep close to me."

We picked up our bundles, slung the shields over our shoulders, and set off.

The path started out dry but soon became soggy. Sometimes the water came up to our ankles, other times we walked on spongy ground or found ourselves waist high in weeds. We travelled throughout the morning, but the Tor stayed stubbornly distant. At noon, the sun had burned off the haze and the day turned warm. We stopped briefly for a lunch of bread and cheese, then continued toward the Tor.

"Many years ago," Malcolm said, "this used to be a lake. The Tor rose from its centre, majestic and mysterious, and the only way to reach it was by boat."

"How long ago was that?" I asked.

"A long time," Malcolm said. "Hundreds of years."

"So, no one can follow us," Mitch said. "I mean, anyone who doesn't know the path."

Malcolm kept walking, picking his way toward the distant mound. "It is true that few could follow us this way," he said. "But the land is firmer to the south. That is the way Reinhart will come. As will Falan and Lubbik. The roads they took will lead them there."

I felt a flutter of panic when I realized we were heading to the same place where Reinhart was, or would soon be. The only comfort I could find was that we were on the opposite side, where he couldn't see us.

After a few hours, the ground grew firmer, the shadows longer and, in the late afternoon, we reached the base of the Tor.

Up close, it didn't seem very large, more like a hill than a mountain. It was the flat land around it that lent it the illusion of height, and yet there was something other-worldly about it, standing, as it did, alone in such a broad plain. It also didn't look like a normal hill. It was sorta teardrop shaped, and had ridges, that appeared to be a path, running horizontally around its slope. Thick shrubs lined the path, blocking access to it and keeping us from climbing straight up. Malcolm led us around the base, to a point where there was an opening.

"This was the path maze," Malcolm said. "To gain the top of the Tor, you had to follow it, winding seven times around the sides of the Tor until you reached the top."

"Do you think Reinhart knows the way?" I asked, taking a step forward. Malcolm put a hand on my arm.

"You will find," he said, "when we come to the south side, that the maze has been breached. We can go up the slope directly from there. It will be easier and faster, but it will also allow our foes an advantage. We can only hope, if Reinhart has tracked us here, that he is waiting for us at the top."

"Why?"

"Because we are not going to the top," Malcolm said. "We are going to the chamber of the Talisman."

We quickened our pace, following Malcolm as he led us around the Tor to the south side. There, as predicted, we found a path cut through the maze, leading up the slope. We scrambled from level to level, clawing our way up the steep incline, from one path to the next. On the fifth level, Malcolm stopped.

"This is where the entrance to the chamber is," he said. "We must be cautious. Follow me."

Slowly, we moved along the path and soon came to what appeared to be a large crack in the hill. Here Malcolm stopped. The split—a large, inverted V that looked like the mouth of a cave—was a scar on the otherwise placid tor. Next to it was a large, egg-shaped rock. Both looked out of place.

"The entrance to the Chamber is open," Malcolm said. "We may be too late."

He ran toward it, and we followed. When we reached the gap, I saw it opened onto a rough stone stairway, leading down into darkness. Lying on the top step, his throat slit, was Lubbik. Blood pooled around his open neck and dripped down the steps.

Malcolm knelt next to the body and touched a finger to the blood. I thought he might be meditating on his former friend, and how he had come to this end, but all he said was, "This is fresh. Falan is not far ahead of us. Quickly."

He stepped over Lubbik and descended the stairs. "Come," he said.

Careful to avoid stepping on Lubbik or his blood, we followed Malcolm. The stones were worn with age and the only sound was our footsteps and the occasional drip of water. At the base of the stairs, a passageway led further into the Tor. It should have been pitch black, but the walls glowed with a dim green light that didn't exactly allow us to see, but at least guided our way.

"The Talisman is still in place," Malcolm said, running his hand over the glowing wall. "We are not yet too late. Hurry."

We ran down the corridor, which angled downward in a sweeping curve. As the end of the tunnel came in sight, I saw more green light, but glowing brighter, in what seemed to be a large room. We rushed toward it and, when the corridor ended and we entered the room, I stopped and gasped in amazement.

The room was large as a cathedral, with a vaulted ceiling and stone pillars, and everything glowed with that eerie green light, so there were no shadows. It made me feel strange, like I was looking through murky water. I ran to the centre of the room, between the rows of pillars, where we could see an altar carved into the far wall. On top of the altar stood a giant cross, intricately engraved with loops and interwoven ropes. I recognized it as a Celtic cross, and in its centre was the Talisman, making a black hole where the arms met. It you left out the engravings and just drew an outline, it would look very much like the image Mitch had carved into Garberund's table.

In front of the altar, wearing our cloak, was Falan. He was climbing up it, grasping at the cross, his arm stretching up, ready to take the Talisman.

"Falan!" Malcolm's voice echoed through the chamber. Falan froze, then he turned slowly to face us, pulling the cloak aside so we could see his sword and dagger. "An old man and two peasants? I've already dispatched one old man; I can handle another. And your so-called knights will give me no trouble."

"You know as well as I do that they are Guardians of the Talisman, and more than a match for you."

Me and Mitch stepped away from Malcolm, our shields in front of us, moving slowly toward Falan.

"Oh, they could give me trouble," Falan said, "but as soon as I have the Talisman, I will be invincible."

"You do not understand," Malcolm said. "The Talisman does not protect a person. Taking it to William will not guarantee his victory. But if you remove it, you will break the bond, its power will diminish, and the Land will be in danger."

Falan snorted. "Lubbik spouted that nonsense to me, as well. All his ancient myths and legends." He turned back to the cross, reached up and grabbed the Talisman.

"Falan!" Malcolm cried. "This is bigger than you. Bigger than Harold and William. If you care at all about the Land, about the people, about people not yet born, do not remove the Talisman."

I saw Mitch move forward, and I moved to match his speed. I assumed the plan was to crush Falan between our shields, like we had with the thief, only Falan wasn't on the ground, he was on the altar, and we'd have to climb to reach him. But that didn't stop me, or Mitch. We'd have to figure out what to do when we got there. Then I saw something that made me hesitate. Leaning against one of the columns was a sword, an old sword, in a leather scabbard, with a belt attached. Both the scabbard and belt were crumbling with age, and the handle of the sword was corroded, but it was a weapon. I lunged toward it as Mitch reached the base of the altar and Falan plucked the Talisman from its setting in the centre of the cross.

Then everything went black.

Chapter 39

Mitch

I rushed ahead as Charlie fell behind. I couldn't hesitate; there was no time. Falan reached up to the cross, his hand hovering over the Talisman. I raised my shield, ready to strike at his shins with the metal edge. They were within easy reach, and I planned to hit him hard enough to break both his ankles.

But his hand moved, and the vast room went suddenly dark.

It wasn't the blackness that stopped me, it was the screaming.

A piercing shriek came from every direction, paralysing me. Not a cry of pain, but a wail of anguish that came from deep within the ground and through the walls. It tore at me, weighing me down with sorrow. I tried to keep going, but found myself on the floor, feeling cold, hard rock beneath my hands and knees. I struggled to rise, but the screaming continued, and a sadness so all-consuming gripped me, making me convulse with sobs.

I don't know how long it continued. A minute? An hour? It couldn't have been that long because I would have died of heartsickness. All I know is, the wailing gradually stopped, but the pervading feeling of sadness stayed. I gulped stale air, trying to regain control of myself, then felt for my shield and strapped it on my back. Falan would be long gone by now, and we had to find him. I rose to my feet, still feeling shaky.

Charlie would be somewhere behind me, and Malcolm further away. I held my hands out in front of me, totally blind, feeling my way forward.

"Charlie, where are you?"

I stepped forward. My hand brushed against someone.

"Charlie?"

But a hand grabbed my arm and twisted it behind my back. Then I felt the point of a knife at my throat.

Chapter 40

Charlie

The blackness was absolute. I froze, bewildered, wondering what to do. Then the cavern filled with a high-pitched moan so piercing, so mournful, so anguished, that I fell to the floor, curled into a ball, and covered my ears. It did no good. The shriek came from the pillars, from the walls, from the floor, from the land itself. It filled my head, blocking out every other sound, including my own screams.

Slowly, the sound subsided. I lay still, exhausted, listening, staring into the blackness. A rustling and clanking of metal sounded in the dark. I sat up.

"Charlie!" Mitch's voice.

"Mitch," I called. "Are you all right?"

But it was Falan who answered. "I have him. He can't talk right now because he has a knife at his throat."

Then Malcolm's voice came from some distance away. "Don't hurt him."

"Oh, I wouldn't do that. At least not yet. He's far too valuable. Now you and the other one, move to one side. Both of you. Quickly or I'll slit his throat."

"I'm going, I'm going," I said. "Mitch, are you okay?"

Mitch's voice, small and shaking, came through the darkness. "I'm sorry. I thought I could stop him."

"No," I said, "it was my fault. I hesitated. I saw—"

"Malcolm," Falan shouted." Where are you?"

"I'm moving," Malcolm said. His voice travelled close to where I was. "Charlie, come to me."

"But Mitch—"

"Your brother's life depends on you doing as Malcolm suggested," Falan said. "Go to him. Stand with him. Do nothing and your brother might live."

A strangled cry came through the darkness. I groped my way toward Malcolm. "I'm here," I called. "Malcolm, where are you."

A hand landed on my shoulder. "Here," Malcolm said. "We are together now, Falan. Release him."

I heard shuffling and muffled cries. Then, from the end of the chamber where the entrance corridor was, Falan spoke. "You will stay in here until I am well away. I am taking him with me as protection. If I see you leave the cavern, I will kill him. If I discover you are following me, I will kill him. Do you understand?"

"Yes," Malcolm said. "We do."

"Good." Falan's voice echoed from inside the corridor. "If I don't see you before I reach William, I will release the boy. That is a promise."

"Mitch," Malcolm said, his voice echoing in the vast chamber, "remember Lubbik."

Falan's voice came back from deeper in the tunnel, "Wise advice." Mitch yelped, then Falan spoke again. "Did you hear and understand? You remain alive only as long as you remain useful."

Then, so quietly I could barely hear, Mitch said, "Yes, I understand."

Their footsteps grew dim and distant.

"Falan," Malcolm called after them. "The Talisman will not give you what you want."

But Falan did not answer. All we heard was silence. I tried to rush forward but Malcolm's hand gripped my shoulder.

"Keep still," Malcolm said.

"But we need to save Mitch." I thrashed and struggled but Malcolm held tight.

"If you want your brother to live, you must stay calm. If we rush out now, Falan will surely hear us, and I do not believe he was bluffing. You saw what he did to Lubbik."

"But we have to go after them."

"When the time is right. For now, we wait."

I stopped struggling and took a deep breath. "How long."

"A few more minutes, then we will go to the opening, and wait there."

"But we will go after them. There has to be a way. We can track them, sneak up at night and … there's a sword. I saw a sword leaning against a pillar." I struggled again, trying to break loose."

"We will follow. Prudently. So, they will not know we are there."

"But that won't get us close enough. Falan will kill Mitch anyway. He's not going to let him go. Let me get the sword so we'll at least have a chance of freeing him."

Malcolm held me tight and leaned close to my ear. "Forget the sword. Focus on Mitch and keeping him alive."

I let myself go limp, but Malcolm still held tight. "Come. Let's go to the entrance now. Carefully."

My mind was still on the sword, but Malcolm guided me forward, into the corridor leading to the outside. Soon we could see dim light ahead and, at length, we came to the stone stairway. As we neared the top, we found the body of Lubbik, still lying near the entrance.

"Help me carry him down to the corridor," Malcolm said. "We will lay him out there. It is the least he deserves."

We half carried, half slid Lubbik down the stone steps. I was glad that Malcolm let me take the feet instead of having to hold his body by the shoulders, with his head flopping hideously on his neck. We laid him next to the wall, covered his face with his cloak, and went back up the steps.

Peering over the top step, I saw Falan, wearing our cloak, and Mitch, still wearing his shield, both on horseback, making their way over the soggy path. Mitch was balanced precariously on his horse, his hands bound behind his back, his horse tethered to Falan's, who turned to look over his shoulder every few minutes to make sure we weren't following. I ducked down every time he turned, even though I doubted he could see me from such a distance. When I dared to lift my head up again, they were always further away.

When they were nearly out of sight, I started to crawl out of the opening.

"We need to go now, or we'll lose them."

"Wait, Charlie," Malcolm said, reaching for me again.

I darted away from him. "You wait," I said. "He's not your brother."

"Charlie!"

I ducked behind a row of shrubs and peered out at the distant figures of Falan and Mitch. Falan was not looking back as often, so I skidded down the slope to the next level, checked, and slid down again, ducking behind a row of shrubs. Turning back, I could just see the top of the doorway to the underground, still open. Malcolm was nowhere to be seen, but that didn't mean he wasn't sneaking up on me. I checked the road once more. Mitch and Falan were nearly out of sight. I had to move quick. Then I heard the thud of heavy footsteps behind me. A hand gripped my shoulder and I tried to shrug it off. "Malcolm, let me go."

But the hand spun me around and another gripped my throat and I found myself staring into the face of Reinhart. Behind him stood Hoban, Blekwulf and Gerwald with grins on their faces.

"So," Reinhart said, "Malcolm is here?"

"No, no he's not," I said. "I left him some time ago. Falan has Mitch and I ran ahead to rescue him. It's just me here. Look, there's Falan. With Mitch."

Reinhart looked into the distance. "And so it is. Such a disappointment. I was looking forward to killing both of you. I am certain Lord Falan must have his reasons, but I have mine, as well. Now where is Malcolm?"

"I told you, he's—"

Reinhart shook me so hard I had to clench my jaw to keep my teeth from rattling together.

"Next lie and you die here and now," Reinhart said, pulling a dagger. "I want Malcolm." He pressed the blade against my throat. "Go ahead, lie to me."

I heard a deep rumble and felt the ground shake under my feet. It spread to the entire hillside, causing Reinhart's men to look around nervously. Reinhart, however, kept his grip tight and his knife at my throat. The tremor grew so strong I was afraid he might slit my throat by accident. I glanced up again, just in time to see the top of the opening slide closed. Then

215

Malcolm stepped into view.

"Do not hurt him," he said, his voice carrying over the fading rumble.

Reinhart glanced up at him and lowered the knife. "It seems luck is still with you," he said, though I wasn't sure if he meant to say it to me or Malcolm, "but don't worry, it will run out soon enough."

Hoban, Blekwulf and Gerwald gaped at him but made no move. Reinhart pointed up the slope, the dagger still in his hand. "After him, you cowering women," he bellowed. "He's there. Take him."

The three of them began scrambling up the slope, but Malcolm walked down to them. Despite his surrender, they flung him to the ground and dragged him forward, to where Reinhart was holding me.

"Well," Reinhart said. "I guess we have as many as we are going to get. Now to bring you back for your executions."

Chapter 41

Mitch

"Remember Lubbik," I thought, as we trotted along the road.

It was awkward sitting on the horse with my hands tied behind my back, especially with the shield on. It bounced against my wrists and the weight of it kept making me feel like I was falling over backward. We weren't going fast, but Falan wasn't exactly taking a stroll through the park. He had the horses going at a fast walk, which bounced me painfully in the saddle and threatened to make me fall off.

"Remember Lubbik."

Falan looked over his shoulder again to make sure we weren't being followed, and to be certain I was still with him. He rode with the cloak wrapped around him, and the Talisman in a leather bag on his belt, the prize he had stolen, which he would now bring to William. Charlie and Malcolm could chase after us, but they couldn't stop Falan. With me as a hostage, Falan was safe. That made me useful, and if I was useful, I was safe.

"Remember Lubbik."

Lubbik was dead because he had ceased being useful. But before Falan had been able to dispose of him, he had unwittingly helped us by slowing Falan down. Now Falan needed me. Could I turn that into an advantage, like Lubbik did? I couldn't stop Falan, but I could hobble him. Perhaps enough to allow Charlie and Malcolm to catch up.

"Remember Lubbik."

I looked down. The ground looked hard and far away.

"Remember Lubbik."

I let myself fall from the saddle.

Chapter 42

Charlie

Gerwald took my shield and tied my hands in front of me. They bound Malcolm in the same way and forced us down the hill, falling, slipping, rolling, until, by the time we reached the bottom, I was bruised and aching.

With long ropes, they tied us to Gerwald's horse and set out on the muddy track that Falan and Mitch had travelled. I struggled to keep on my feet as we ran behind the horse; I knew if I fell Gerwald would just drag me, and I didn't want that.

Malcolm looked weary, and he too struggled to stay upright. I wanted to apologize, but didn't dare speak for fear I would lose my concentration and slip.

We joined a firmer road, which made the going easier, but with each step I grew more and more weary. Sometime later, as the sun was low in the sky, and just when I was sure I couldn't take another step, Reinhart led us off the road and into a field.

There they dismounted and began making camp, leaving me and Malcolm tied to Gerwald's horse. Reinhart and his men paid us no attention, so I collapsed on the grass, gasping. Soon, Malcolm sat next to me, keeping his eye on Reinhart and his men.

"I'm sorry," I said, when I was able to breathe normally. "I should have listened."

"You did what you thought was right," Malcolm said, not taking his eyes off Reinhart. "You showed loyalty and bravery, and for that you must not be sorry."

"But I got us into this mess. Now we'll never rescue Mitch, or get the cloak back. I've ruined everything. You suspected Reinhart was out there. I should have listened."

Malcolm turned and looked at me. "Wisdom and caution come with age. For now, you must make do with loyalty and bravery."

"But what good—"

"Hush now. Rest. There is nothing else we can do."

He watched as Blekwulf made a fire, Hoban put on a pot to boil and Gerwald tended the horses. Eventually, Blekwulf came to us and re-tied our hands behind our backs, lashed our legs together and secured us to a tree so we couldn't hop away in the night. Then the four of them sat around the fire to eat whatever it was that Hoban had made. I doubted they were going to offer us any. They hadn't even given us any water, and my throat felt like sandpaper.

Whatever Hoban had made, there didn't appear to be much of it, and it didn't appear to be very good. Gerwald sputtered when he took his first spoonful, and they all, Hoban included, ate grimly. When they started to argue, however, it wasn't about the state of the food. It was about us.

"But they will slow us down," Blekwulf said. "What is more important? Getting to the battle on time or impressing the men with another execution."

"It's not about the men," Reinhart said, "Harold wants them."

"And would Harold rather see us at the battle,"

Gerwald said, "or arrive late with prisoners he no longer needs?"

Reinhart dropped his bowl, still half-full of Hoban's slop, on the ground. "That is the problem. We don't know how much time we have. We could easily arrive before the battle with no prisoners. That would displease Harold as well."

"I agree," Blekwulf said, "but whatever our condition, arriving before the battle is most important, and we have a better chance of doing that without them."

Reinhart sat silent, staring into the fire. Malcolm leaned toward me and whispered, in a strangely loud voice, "Their condition would improve if they were better fed."

This broke Reinhart's rumination. He stood, looking our way, with his hand on his sword. "Blekwulf speaks true. We kill them now, ride hard and find Harold before the battle." He kicked the bowl at his feet, sending it rolling, spilling its contents across the grass. "But first, our prisoners will feed us a proper meal."

My stomach dropped and I was glad I was sitting down because my knees would surely have buckled. Malcolm, however, appeared calm.

"I am no longer your cook," he said, "I am your prisoner. And you plan to execute me, so I have no incentive to do your bidding."

Reinhart came toward us, drawing his sword. "I'll give you incentive." He stopped in front of us, the tip of his sword aimed at my throat. If I hadn't been so dehydrated, every bit of moisture in my body would have leaked out.

"Would you like to see this one hung by his feet and

flayed alive, a little at a time?"

Malcolm looked my way, his face serene. "I would not."

"Then cook for us."

Malcolm nodded. "I will need to be freed and allowed to gather."

Reinhart glared at Malcolm. I could sense he was wrestling with his suspicion and his desire for a decent meal.

"Let him go," Gerwald called. "If he fails to return, he will still hear this one's cries."

"And then we can eat him," Hoban added.

Reinhart sheathed his sword. "Very well. Be quick about it."

◆

Every second that Malcolm was gone, I watched Gerwald—who was sitting by the fire, sharpening his axe and leering at me—wondering how long would be too long. Did Reinhart have a set time in mind, or would they just wait until they were bored? The sun was sinking lower. Surely, they wouldn't wait past twilight.

But Malcolm returned in a short time, carrying three rabbits on a stick and a sack bulging with greens. He went directly to the fire and set everything out as if it was a normal day.

"I can work faster if I have my assistant," was all he said.

Reinhart and the others stood around him, saying nothing, but Reinhart nodded, and Hoban came to untie me. I went to Malcolm and knelt by his side.

"Skin these," he said, tossing the rabbits my way, "and cut up the meat." He looked up at Reinhart. "And we will need water."

Reinhart sighed and inclined his head toward Hoban and Blekwulf.

In the end, Gerwald skinned the rabbit, because I was making a mess of it. I chopped the roots Malcolm had gathered and watched the pot as it began to boil. Then Malcolm mixed everything together, along with some barley Hoban had in his saddle bag.

As the stew boiled, Malcolm seasoned it with herbs from his bag, carefully measuring out ingredients, crushing the dried leaves between his fingers and sprinkling it into the pot. Soon my stomach was rumbling as the savoury scents drifted through the camp. I knew I wasn't going to get any, though. I put that thought out of my mind, and concentrated on the stew, not what was going to happen after it.

As soon as the stew was simmering, Reinhart and his men sat around the fire, with bowls ready. Malcolm served them, then sat next to me while we watched them eat and my stomach churned.

They seemed to be enjoying it. Malcolm served them seconds and was soon scraping the bottom of the pot. They scooped up the last from their bowls, not paying much attention to us and I wondered if that was Malcolm's plan. But he didn't appear ready to run while they were otherwise occupied, so maybe he was thinking they would find us—or at least him—too valuable to kill. If that was his plan, it didn't work.

"Excellent stew, Malcolm," Reinhart said, looking up from his empty bowl. "I am going to miss you."

Hoban ran a finger around his bowl and stuck it in his mouth. "Is there any more in the pot?"

"No," Blekwulf said. "You ate it all."

Hoban threw his bowl at him. "I? You had three

223

bowls yourself."

"That's enough," Reinhart said, looking my way. "We still have a job to do."

"This is too good to waste," Blekwulf said, grabbing the pot and scraping his spoon around the bottom. "Too bad there's not enough to share."

"Leave it," Reinhart said.

Gerwald threw his bowl at Blekwulf. "I don't need more food. I need my axe."

Blekwulf laughed and threw his bowl, and the pot, at Gerwald.

"Enough of this," Reinhart said, but his voice had lost its ability to command. Malcolm, still sitting began moving away from the fire. I did the same.

"Stay where you are," Reinhart shouted.

Gerwald and Blekwulf were now giggling and slapping at each other. Reinhart looked their way and then back at Malcolm. "You … you …" He struggled to his feet and drew his sword, but instead of holding it high, he dragged it behind him. He took a few shambling steps in our direction, then he crumpled to the ground. Just beyond the fire, Blekwulf, Hoban and Gerwald were lying on their backs, snoring.

I blinked, unable to believe what I was seeing. "What did you do?" I whispered, afraid I might wake them.

"A potion of herbs to put them to sleep," Malcolm said, getting to his feet. "Hurry now, they will not sleep forever."

After taking my shield back from Reinhart—being careful not to wake him—we untied the horses and led them from the campsite. Then we mounted and rode away, leading the riderless horses behind us. We made good time on the road, giving me hope that we might catch up with Falan, but then Malcolm left the road and led us into a vast, rolling prairie of low shrubs and grass. By now it was getting dark, but we walked the horses for a few more miles, then stopped.

"Go through their bags," Malcolm said. "Throw out anything that will not be necessary."

All I found were a few blankets, two water skins, some stale bread, and a short knife. We drank the water, ate the bread, and let the excess horses go. Then we took the blankets and laid down in the grass. The sky was clear, and, despite the blankets, I shivered against the cold night. Then I thought of Mitch and shivered harder.

"How are we going to find my brother?" I asked, staring up into the stars as if they could give me an answer.

But it was Malcolm who responded. "The same way Huscarl Reinhart found us. We do not know Falan's route, but we know his destination. He will bring the Talisman to William."

"But how will we find William?"

"That is easy. Follow the destruction; William will be at the end of it."

Chapter 43

Mitch

I woke the next morning with the sun on my face, wondering if it was the last sunrise I would see. Despite the sun, I shivered with cold, uncomfortable under my thin blanket, with my hands and feet bound and staked to the ground with a length of rope. My body ached from the falls from my horse, though that had stopped after a few hours when Falan, perhaps realizing what I was up to, let me ride with my hands untied.

We rode hard and long, stopping only when it became too dark for the horses to see. Falan made me tend to them and tether them in a stand of trees. Then he tied me up again, trussing me up like a Christmas turkey and staking me to the ground. I lay watching him as he sat by the fire, as his hand moved furtively toward his belt, wondering if he was going to take out his knife. Instead, he removed the bag that held the Talisman. I thought he'd take it out, but he merely rubbed it in his hands, feeling the Talisman through the leather. He sat there a long time, attempting either to find the courage or overcome the temptation, to take the Talisman out and gaze into it.

He pressed the bag between his hands, rubbing it with his palms, feeling the black stone within. But he didn't try to take it out.

Then he saw me watching him.

"You want me to hold it," he said. "You want me to look into the Talisman."

I shook my head. "I want you to release me. Beyond that, I don't care what you do."

He stood and came to me. "You do wish it." He knelt next to me. "You wish it to kill me."

"The stone won't kill you," I said.

"You saw what happened when I removed it from the cross. If it truly has the powers that Lubbik spoke of, it could certainly strike a man down." He leaned close, his wild eyes glaring into mine and his foul breath warm against my face. "You are a Guardian of the Talisman. Tell me what you know."

"I know you will not benefit from looking into it," I said. "You need to be chosen."

"And you think I am not?" He pulled at the rope binding my hands. When they were free, he dumped the Talisman out of the bag. "Take it up. Take it up and look into it."

It was awkward, lying on my back with a rope around my middle, but I raised it up to where I could see it and tried to calm myself. I didn't go in deeply, as I had other times, which I was grateful for. All I saw was water. A wide stream of flowing water. A field. A hill. Then Falan snatched it away.

"What did you see"

"Water," I said, as he re-tied my hands.

Falan shook his head. "And you call yourself a Guardian, one of the Chosen. The Talisman does not favour you."

He returned to the fire. I saw he hadn't put the Talisman back in the bag. He was holding it in his hands, turning it over, rubbing the smooth surface. He glanced my way, a look of fury on his face, then he held the Talisman up and gazed into it.

Nothing happened for a moment, and I wondered if he was going to be one of those for whom the Talisman is nothing but a black mirror. But then his eyes widened, and his jaw went slack, and I knew the Talisman was speaking to him. His expression did not change to one of horror, or confusion, nor did he cry out or call for help. Instead, his lips curled into a grin that looked more like a grimace, and I knew his dark heart had connected with the beautiful side of the Talisman, the side that told you, not the truth, but the lies you wanted to hear.

What would Falan want, I wondered. Money, power? They were the things that men like him most coveted. Or did he want more? To be king? To be safe? This last thought worried me. If Falan was worried about Malcolm and Charlie catching up with us, and the Talisman convinced him they would not, then I would no longer be useful.

I watched, but he gave no sign. He simply kept staring into the black stone, his lips pulled into an expression of ecstasy. I watched until the night grew cold, and the fire burned low. He had thrown a blanket down near me and I struggled to reach it, and struggled more to cover myself with it. I wasn't worried about him hearing, he was totally focused on the Talisman. I watched as the moon rose. I watched as my eyes grew heavy. I watched as I snapped awake hours later and saw him, sitting in front of the cold ashes, the stone still clutched in his hands. I watched. And then I slept.

And now it was morning. Not early morning, for I felt the sun, warm on my face, which meant it would have been light enough to start riding hours ago. Was Falan still looking into the Talisman? Or was he getting ready to slit my throat? I opened my eyes. The fire was out. The embers stone cold. And Falan was gone.

◆

It took nearly an hour to work myself free, and it was only that quick because I didn't have to worry about Falan hearing me. I grunted and squirmed and strained and bucked and finally got one hand loose. After that, it was easy.

I went to where I had tethered the horses and found he had taken only one, and only his saddle. He had left his saddle bags, my saddle and, I was relieved to see, my shield. He must have still been in a trance, or in a hurry. Either way, I was free, and hungry.

I ate and drank and stared at the fire pit, wondering what to do.

Charlie and Malcolm might be coming, but they might not find me, or they might take too long. Falan was going somewhere in a hurry, and if we didn't follow him now, we would never catch him. And he had the Talisman, and our cloak.

By the time I finished eating, I had made my decision. I saddled the horse and followed Falan. It wasn't hard. He was in too much of a hurry to cover his tracks. There was a path through the tall grass, and when I came to any roads, I knew which direction he would be going in. It seemed common sense, and simple deduction, but after a while I felt it might be more. Perhaps the Talisman was guiding me, keeping me on track. If that was so, I hoped it would do the same for Malcolm and Charlie.

I rode as fast as I dared, mindful that I couldn't get another horse. But the one I had was young and strong and seemed up to the task. I rode and rested and camped under the stars and, on the fifth day, I came to the first ruined village.

Chapter 44

Charlie

We rose early, before sun-up, ate what little food we had and set off. It was a chilly morning and I felt stiff and cold from sleeping on the ground. The horses were not happy, either, having been woken earlier than usual. They whinnied and kicked, and the ride was rough. But at least it helped me stay awake.

We rode as the sun climbed high, then we stopped to rest the horses. During the long afternoon, as the sun began to descend, we rode through a seemingly endless sea of grass that rippled in the breeze like brown waves. We didn't stop for dinner because we had no food left. All we could do was find water for ourselves and the horses, and jettison anything we didn't need, which Malcolm told me was everything.

"It will make it easier on the horses," he said, when I objected. "They are tired and need all the comfort we can give them."

"But what about us? We've got no blankets. What are we going to sleep on tonight?"

"Do not fear," was all he said, "necessities come to those who need them." Then we got back on the horses and continued riding.

We only had a few hours of daylight left to us, and the endless prairie stretched on and on. Then, as twilight neared, I saw something on the horizon. We headed toward it, and a strange feeling of déjà vu overcame me. Gradually, the figure took on a familiar shape. It was a stone sculpture, in the middle of a sea of grass. But not a sculpture, really, more like a temple, but then, not really a temple, either.

"That's the sacred place," I said, pointing toward the grey stones, "what we call Stonehenge. You brought us here, me and Mitch, and Talan was with us, And Kayla. It was where you … you."

Malcolm nodded. "Then you know there is a settlement not far from here, where we will find food and rest." He winked at me. "And blankets."

We rode past the massive ring of stones. It was almost the same as when we had been there last time. There were a few more stones lying on the ground, and from what I could see of the inner circle, it looked as if there was only one altar there now, but it was otherwise unchanged.

We circled around the structure and found a path, so narrow we had to ride single file. The path, too, felt familiar, and I realized it was the road to Sarum.

"These stones, this path," I said, "they are so familiar it feels like I've stepped back in time."

Malcolm, riding ahead of me, nodded. "As indeed you have."

It was dusk by the time we reached Sarum, and we were met by guards as we approached the settlement. They challenged us, readying arrows and drawing their bows, but once they saw Malcolm, who they seemed familiar with, they put down their weapons and led us to the village. Sarum still sat on a fortified hill, inside a huge ring of earth, so it took a while to get there. By the time we crossed the bridge and were admitted through the gate, it was nearly dark.

An old man in a robe came to greet us. Our horses were taken and tended to, the old man embraced Malcolm and then came to me. I expected he would greet me the same way he had Malcolm, but instead he raised his hands and looked up at the darkened sky.

"A Guardian of the Talisman," he said. "I thank the Land I have been blessed to see this."

I didn't know what to say to that, so I just nodded.

We were led through the streets, and others came out, greeting Malcolm, who they clustered around. After speaking with him for a minute or so, they would turn to me and stare. I was never certain if they were afraid of me, or just awestruck.

I was too tired to care. The only thing I felt was relief when I was led into a single-room hut containing a small fire and primitive bed. Food and water were also there, on a low table, and I was invited to stay and do whatever I wished. And what I wished, despite how hungry I felt, was sleep.

◆

The next morning, I was taken to a larger hut where Malcolm and three other men—all with grey hair and beards—sat at a long table eating breakfast. I joined them, even though I had just eaten the food left for me the night before. When our breakfast was over, I felt as rested, refreshed, and relaxed as I had since I'd arrived. But then Malcolm told our hosts that our journey was urgent and that ended my relaxation.

The elders picked horses for us, good, strong ones with sturdy saddles and new bridles. I was provided with new clothes and shoes, and someone had polished my shield until it gleamed. Food and blankets were packed into saddle bags and arranged on the horses.

Then Malcolm appeared, wearing new clothes, and carrying a staff and a small pack. He put the pack into his saddle bags and mounted, holding the staff. The elders and some of the townspeople walked with us as we headed out of Sarum to the gates of the village.

As we started across the bridge, the others stayed behind, wishing us a good journey. Malcolm turned and saluted them, raising his staff. And then we rode on.

I felt buoyed by a sound night's sleep and a full stomach, but as I gazed at the land stretching out before us, and realized that Mitch and Falan could be anywhere, or nowhere, my confidence dimmed, and I wondered, not for the first time, if I was ever going to make it back home.

Chapter 45

Mitch

Days of riding meant days of boredom, which gave me a lot of time to think. The only thing of consequence I had been able to determine with any certainty, however, was what day it was. And I had only been able to work that out because I'd heard two of Harold's officers arguing about the recent battle. They were discussing how they could best celebrate their valour to make the maximum impression on the people back home, but the only thing they could agree on was the date, which they said was the twenty-fifth of September. By carefully counting the days since then, I had arrived at several different conclusions, but I had a lot of time to think it over, and the date I eventually decided on was the thirteenth of October. I had no idea what day of the week it was, but my money was on Friday, because ever since we'd been here, apart from those brutally hot days in York, the weather had been mostly agreeable, and now, it was raining.

That meant I couldn't push my horse. If we rode too fast, she might slip and hurt herself and that would be the end. I had no hope that it would slow Falan down, however, as he wouldn't care what happened to his horse.

Near noon, when the rain was at its hardest, I smelled what I thought might be someone cooking a meal. More specifically, it was the damp scent of doused coals, with a hint of barbecued beef. Then, in the distance, I saw a plume of black smoke. I headed toward it. If it was a village, I might be able to barter for food, or even trade my horse for another, well-rested one. There was, of course, no reason to believe they would, but I was hoping that my strange ways, and my shield, might convince them I was someone important, who they might feel honoured to do business with.

As I drew nearer, the smell of stale smoke and seared meat mingled with an unpleasant scent of decay, and when I arrived at the village, I found it was nothing but a collection of half a dozen houses and a scattering of barns, and all of them had been burned to the ground.

Two of the barns, despite the rain, were still smouldering, sending black smoke into the dark sky. Their walls had been knocked down, leaving rectangles of jagged, soot-blackened stone. Heaped within, jumbles of thick beams and mounds of matted hay glowed orange, and entwined in the wreckage, sizzling on the hot embers, lay the carcasses of three or four cows. Other animals, and a few people, lay scattered among the ruins. There was not a living soul—human or animal—in sight.

My horse shied away, not wishing to approach any closer. I didn't force her; I didn't want to go near it, either. So, I circled around until I found what I was looking for: hoof-prints. Dozens of them. They had come in along a narrow road and left the same way. To the east.

I urged my horse forward, following them.

By mid-afternoon the rain had stopped, and soon

after the clouds began to part, and I had found two more ruined villages. Both were larger than the first, and both had survivors, huddling in what shelter they could fashion from the wreckage. In the first, a small group of women and children sat around a fire under a makeshift lean-to, cooking something in a big pot. At the edge of the village, I saw three men digging holes next to a pile of what looked like rags. When I got closer, I realized it was a stack of bodies. They paid no attention to me as I rode by.

The second village came into view as the sky cleared and the sun sank low. White smoke revealed its location and, once again, I found nothing but ruin. Only a handful of woman and children remained, sitting in the mud, sheltering against one of the few remaining walls. They were covered in mud, their clothing and hair in disarray, their eyes wide and empty. They looked at me with disinterest as I approached, and when I asked who had done this, they merely pointed to the east. I left them what food I had and rode on.

I rode until the sun set and the light faded, then stopped near a stream so my horse could drink and graze. I found dry ground under the boughs of a pine tree and slept. The next morning, early, I set off again, heading into the sun. I saw the smoke from more burned villages but didn't go near. I had seen enough.

Far in the distance, near the horizon, more smoke rose into the morning air. It couldn't have been a village, it had to be a city, it was so large. And it wasn't the dark smoke of a ransacked town, it reminded me of the haze over London when we had passed by on our way north.

I headed toward it, urging my horse to move faster

over the rolling grassland. As the sun climbed high, I heard a strange sound, a distant rumble that rose and fell. Then, on the crest of the next rise, I saw something black that appeared to be moving. A man, on a horse, heading away from me. As he disappeared over the rise, the sun caught him, and I saw a flash of blue. Our cape. It had to be Falan.

Kicking my horse into a gallop, I chased after him.

Chapter 46

Charlie

For once I was glad it was raining; I didn't want Malcolm to see me cry.

I had endured much during my time here. I had seen Saxons die, I had seen Vikings die, I had even killed some myself, without shedding a tear. But this was different. This was women and children, slaughtered, lying in the mud as the rain splattered down.

Their village had been ransacked, burned, looted. There was nothing left but burned shells, roofless houses, stone walls knocked low and blackened by fire, looking like rotted teeth.

"What happened?" I asked, keeping my face turned away.

"William," Malcolm said. "He needed to give Harold a reason to attack him, and attack him quickly. His hope is that haste and rage will make Harold careless."

I shook my head. "But these people, they're innocent. Women. Children. What purpose—"

"They were simply convenient. There is nothing to be done about it. Our path lies to the east, where soon it will intersect with your brother and Falan. We are both heading for the same destination."

I looked again at the desolation. "Shouldn't we do something? Bury them, get them out of the mud?"

Then my voice cracked. I swallowed back a sob and glanced at Malcolm. "Sorry."

Malcolm sighed. "Do not be. You should only be sorry if such a sight does not stir you to sorrow, or rage."

I looked again at Malcolm, who surveyed the scene calmly. "But …" I trailed off, not wanting to offend him.

He tugged his reins, turning his horse away. "I have seen too much. Pray that you do not. There is nothing we can do here that will help anyone. We must make haste."

We rode away from the village, following a trail of hoof-prints that took us past other villages, most burnt and pillaged, some miraculously intact. Every time we crested a hill I saw, in the distance, plumes of smoke rising over the downs. Soon, the paths we followed became broad, muddy roads where William's army had marched, spreading destruction everywhere they went. The trail wove through the countryside, but always east.

As afternoon approached, the overcast skies cleared, and the sun returned. We rode faster then, galloping through the mud until the sun set and the light left the sky. As night approached, we camped near a stream, beneath a stand of trees.

We rose early the next morning and set off before the sun. At the top of the first down, we stopped to scan the countryside. Stretched out before us, as far as I could see, were misty valleys, hills and trees, and no sign of Mitch or Falan.

"This is hopeless," I said. "We're never going to spot two people in all of this."

"You are right," Malcolm said. "Finding two people

in all of this will be impossible. But finding thousands, that will be easier."

Malcolm looked again into the distance. Then he pointed. "There, can you see?"

I strained my eyes. On the horizon, floating above the dawn haze, was another layer of mist, whiter and wispy, but covering a large area. "What is it?"

"Smoke from the morning fires of thousands of men. That is where the armies are. That is where Falan will take the Talisman. And that is where we must go."

We rode down the hill, heading toward the smoky horizon. The sun rose, grew hot, and sank toward the west. We stopped, letting the horses graze while I climbed a nearby hill to check our progress. The smoky beacon had dispersed, replaced by distant sounds of shouting men, clashing swords and the screaming of horses.

Malcolm stood next to me, his face calm. "This day, we will see battle."

Before we mounted, Malcolm opened his small pack and removed a white druid robe. He put it on and took his staff in his hand. Then he got on his horse, and we rode toward the sound. I knew we were on the right track because it grew louder, giving me hope and filling me with terror at the same time. We galloped closer, bounding through a stand of trees and onto a broad, grassy plain. Not far away, up a rise and beyond a row of low bushes, the two armies were locked in combat.

We headed toward it, pushing our horses to their limit. Then, in the distance, I saw two more horses racing up the rise toward the battle. The lead rider wore a cape that flashed in the sun like a blue flag.

"That's them" I shouted. "Falan and Mitch. They're

just ahead of us."

Chapter 47

Mitch

My only hope was that Falan would fall from his horse in exhaustion.

It had taken more than an hour of hard riding to close the distance between us, and finally, I was only about ten yards behind him, my horse galloping as fast as she could, my shield bouncing painfully on my shoulders. For his part, Falan didn't seem to care that I was gaining on him. He knew I was there—he had glanced over his shoulder, just once—but he didn't seem concerned. He didn't even try to get more speed out of his horse. He just kept galloping, as if he wasn't as tired and hungry as I felt.

Our cloak flapped around him and, occasionally, when it flicked aside, I could see the leather pouch on his belt that held the Talisman. I had no idea what it had shown him, but whatever it was, it gave him determination.

I tried to go faster but my horse, if anything, was slowing down. She had to be near the end of her strength. I patted the side of her neck, trying to encourage her, hoping she could hang on just a little longer.

We galloped over hills, through stands of trees and onto a broad field where the sounds of battle grew loud. I looked up and saw the two warring armies on the far side of the field, just beyond a boundary of low shrubs. I needed to catch him before we got there. I leaned forward and squeezed the horse's flanks with my knees, but she gained no more speed.

The clash of combat loomed closer. It was impossible to tell who was winning, or even who was who. It was simply a chaos of swords, horses, arrows, and men, and even from this distance, the hillside looked red.

Falan spurred his horse, rushing toward the battle, and I followed, struggling to close the gap. But it was no use. I was never going to catch him before he rode into the meat grinder of combat. I was not going have the chance to retrieve the Talisman and our cloak before that, and I wasn't going to get a lucky break.

So, I'd have to make my own luck.

Chapter 48

Charlie

The carnage reminded me of the slaughter of the Vikings. Bodies of men and horses were strewn over the hillside. One army was at the top, protected by a shield wall. I recognized Harold's battle flag flying above their heads, pleased to see that they held the high ground. William's army—mounted men wearing armour and holding shields and long lances—had the disadvantage of attacking uphill. Even as I watched, Williams forces seemed to lose heart and slow their advance.

Just ahead, Falan was charging for William's front line and right behind him was Mitch. It looked as if Falan meant to ride into the battle, which would be suicide. I pushed my horse harder, hoping to reach Mitch before it was too late.

Then, the attacking armies began to drift apart. Harold's shield wall stayed in place but the Norman horsemen, already having slowed, now withdrew, retreating downhill to regroup on a smaller rise not far away. The men in both armies looked weary.

"They are resting," Malcolm said, shouting above the pounding of hooves and the clash of battle. "They will regain their strength and plan their next move."

I didn't know if that was a good thing or not, but I knew it meant Mitch could follow Falan onto the field without being immediately killed. I watched Mitch, mentally urging him forward. If Mitch could catch up to Falan and somehow stop him, me and Malcolm would be on them in minutes. We could take Falan captive, retrieve our cloak, and return the Talisman. All we needed was one lucky break.

Up ahead, Mitch edged closer to Falan. Then his horse stumbled.

Chapter 49

Mitch

Falan's horse slowed as he neared the bushes. I couldn't believe it. I was nearly on him. Then I was flying. I landed in the bushes as Falan's horse leapt over. I glanced back just long enough to see my horse lying on her side, trying to gain her feet. She whinnied and flailed and flopped to the ground, exhausted. My heart ached but there was nothing I could do. I looked toward the battle. The two armies had pulled apart, leaving a widening gap that Falan galloped into, jumping over piles of corpses, discarded weapons, and dead horses. Near the centre of the field, he stopped and turned to face William's troops. With our cloak fluttering regally around him, he pulled the leather sack from his belt and took out the Talisman, holding it up for the men to see.

"I have the Talisman," he said. "Take heart. You cannot lose this battle. I will lead you to victory."

The Norman's cheered and rushed toward him. Then a cry went up from Harold's men as a company of foot soldiers abandoned the shield wall. They charged down the hill to meet William's men. Between the advancing armies, Falan sat on his horse, the Talisman held high, a calm expression on his face.

I ploughed through the bushes and ran toward him, zigzagging across the field, dodging the dead, slipping

247

in blood and gore. I thought of grabbing for a weapon but that would slow me down. I ran faster, getting nearer to Falan as the gap between the raging armies narrowed. Falan wasn't watching the Saxon's, so I came up behind him, jumped as high as I could and grabbed our cloak with both fists. The fastening ripped away and I landed in the mud and blood, holding the cloak in my hands.

Startled, Falan's horse rose onto her hind legs, and Falan, unbalanced and unprepared, fell, landing next to me. For a moment we just stared at each other. Falan's face was contorted with rage, his hand still stretched above his head, clutching the Talisman. That finally prompted me to move. I got up and jumped on Falan's arm, landing on it with both feet. Falan screamed and dropped the Talisman. I scooped it up and, with our cloak draped over my other arm, ran.

Ahead of me, the gap between the armies grew smaller. I had to get off the battlefield or I would be trapped, crushed between them. I ran as fast as I could, the cloak over one shoulder, my shield digging into my back, and the Talisman clutched in my hand. The gap narrowed, but with luck I could make it to the edges of the field before the fighting started. Then a blow to my shoulder sent me reeling. I tripped over a discarded sword and fell, next to its disembowelled owner, with my arms splayed in front of me. The Talisman slipped from my hand and landed three feet away.

Hands groped at the cloak. I pulled away and rolled onto my back. Falan stood above me, a manic gleam in his eyes, his claw-like hands gripping the cloak. I squirmed away and climbed to my feet, but Falan pounced and together we wrestled on the muddy field, scrabbling for the Talisman. I stretched my hand out.

My finger brushed the edge, then the world went dark as Falan pushed my face into the mud. When I looked up, sputtering and gagging, Falan, and the Talisman, were gone.

I jumped to my feet. Falan was racing away, back to his horse, where the armies were nearly upon one another. He attempted to clamber into the saddle, but his horse bolted, leaving him alone on the field. He turned and faced the oncoming Normans, holding the Talisman high for them to see. But they didn't cheer or rally around him. The wall of horsemen, bristling with lances and swords, crashed into the line of Harold's men with a clash of arms and screams of pain. Falan, caught in the middle, was trampled under their feet.

The Talisman flew into the air, spinning like a coin, flashing in the slanting rays of the afternoon sun. I watched it and, for a moment, the world stood still; there was nothing but the blue sky and the winking Talisman. Then it fell, unnoticed, into the maelstrom of battle. I looked away. The gap where I stood was almost gone. The Norman horsemen were nearly upon me. I pulled the shield from my back, threw the cloak over my shoulder, and faced them.

Chapter 50

Charlie

We arrived at the edge of the field in time to see Mitch, with the cloak and the Talisman, running toward us. I shouted and cheered, but then Falan was up, and Mitch went down, and the advancing armies obscured my view.

I kicked my heels into my horse's flanks and snapped the reins. The horse shot forward, leaping the low hedge. Behind me, Malcolm shouted. "No Charlie! It's too late."

Chapter 51

Mitch

I held my shield high, fending off blows from above, dodging left and right, avoiding horses and falling men. Behind me, Harold's men clashed with the cavalry. Wrapping the cloak firmly around my shield arm, I grabbed a sword from the ground and began flailing my way toward them. Shields, swords, lances clashed all around me as horses whinnied and men shouted battle cries or screamed in agony. Soldiers dropped in front of me. Harold's men, William's men, with their arms gone, bellies slit open, or heads cleaved in two.

I stepped over them, swinging my sword, clearing a path, trying to get to Harold's line. A sword flashed. I blocked the blow with my shield, but it knocked me sideways. I planted my feet to keep from slipping on the bloody ground and turned to face my attacker. It was one of Harold's men, a Saxon. He looked at me through glazed eyes, his teeth set in a grimace. Our shields clashed. I shouted but the man took no notice. He wasn't thinking, just fighting. I ducked another slash from his sword. Then he screamed and fell forward, a lance sticking through the centre of his back.

I turned away, swinging my sword at anyone and everything—the horsemen, the Norman foot soldiers, Harold's men. I tried to remember the way to the edge of the field but had lost all sense of direction. And even if I did know where it was, there wasn't any way I could get there.

Then, incredibly, I heard someone calling my name.

I turned around, swinging my sword, screaming, "I'm here! I'm here!"

Then a horse plunged into the fray. On it was Charlie. He reached a hand down. "Come on!"

I dropped my sword and grabbed his hand, but Charlie couldn't hold me, and we both tumbled to the ground. Charlie grabbed for the horse, but it bolted, leaving us both stranded, abandoned on the battlefield.

"Grab a sword," I said, picking up my discarded one.

We stood back-to-back, our shields in front of us, fending off blows, fighting our way toward Harold's men, trying to get to the back of the line, away from the fighting.

An axe swung my way. I deflected it and clashed shields with my attacker. The axe rose again, I raised my sword.

"Mitch?"

"Aelric?"

"Quick, this way!"

We formed a miniature shield wall and fell back behind the Saxon line where the fighting was less intense. I looked across the field and saw that most of Harold's men had withdrawn to their defensive position on the crest of the hill. We were in a pocket of men who were left stranded on a small knoll.

"We're surrounded," Aelric said.

The Normans were coming at us from every direction, squeezing us slowly together. All around, the Saxons and Normans clashed and fell, and our circle grew smaller. I recalled the Viking raiders, after we had outsmarted them, how we had surrounded them, and how they had fought to the last. My heart sank. "They mean to massacre us!"

Then, above the dim of combat, came a shout. At the edge of the battle, Malcolm—wearing a white robe and swinging his staff—galloped through the Norman lines.

I raised my shield. "Malcolm! Over here!"

Chapter 52

Charlie

Malcolm saw us and headed our way, scattering Normans and Saxons alike. "Mitch, to me. Aelric, get a horse. Take Charlie."

Malcolm came beside us and, with one movement, swept Mitch onto the back of his saddle. I dropped my sword and grabbed the reins of a Norman horse while Aelric swung his axe. The rider tumbled to the ground and Aelric jumped into the saddle, pulling me up behind him. Malcolm turned to Mitch. "The Talisman, where is it?"

Mitch pointed to where the battle was at its most ferocious. "There!"

Malcolm turned to look, and for one horrifying moment, I thought we were going to plunge into the fray. But Malcolm turned his head, a sad resignation in his eyes. "Then it is lost. We must warn Harold."

He turned his horse and charged at the Norman line, swinging his staff while Mitch blocked blows with his shield. Behind them, me and Aelric galloped close, rushing forward before the gap closed. We moved fast, surprising the Normans, who seemed either in awe, or frightened, by Malcolm. Either way, they shrank from him, opening a path for us through the carnage. In a few moments, we were behind the line, where a scattering a foot soldiers and horsemen either limped away wounded or waited their turn at the front. We rode through, our horses dodging around the surprised soldiers and trampling over bodies. We headed for the hedge that marked the edge of the field and as we leapt over, I looked behind to see if we were being followed. We weren't.

"Harold must pull back," Malcolm said without slowing his horse. We galloped around the field, heading up the slope of the hill, approaching Harold's army from the rear. We galloped through the support units, the boys watching the supplies, the cooks and cart drivers. Near the top of the hill, the rear guard stood ready to join the fight. We galloped between their ranks.

"Harold," Malcolm shouted.

The fighting was close by. Swords clashed, arrows flew, men screamed. We rode toward the battle flag, and saw Harold on his horse, with his Thegns, fighting beneath it.

Then a shout went up from the Saxons. An arrow had found Harold. I saw it sticking out of Harold's face. From where I was, it looked as if it was in his eye. Blood flowed and Harold dropped his sword. The mounted Normans saw their chance and crashed into the cluster, killing and scattering the Thegns. Then they were upon Harold. I saw the first blow, as a Norman struck Harold's shoulder, nearly cleaving him in two. I looked away.

The Normans overwhelmed the Saxons, crushing their line, slaughtering the weary defenders. Malcolm stopped, and me and Aelric stopped beside him.

"All is lost," Malcolm said. "There is nothing for us but to escape with our lives."

But as we turned our horses, I spied, among the

scattering of retreating Saxons, Reinhart, with Blekwulf, Hoban and Gerwald. Reinhart saw us at the same moment.

"The deserters," Reinhart roared. "Catch them!"

Chapter 53

Mitch

We raced down the hill, Aelric and Charlie, and Malcolm, with me clinging to his robe and hugging my shield and the cloak to my chest. Our horses zig-zagged between the carts, causing startled soldiers to jump out of our way.

"Harold is dead," Malcolm shouted at them. "The Norman's are on their way to slaughter you. Close the gaps. Run for your life."

As we galloped on, I glanced behind, watching the soldiers wheeling the carts together, blocking the way down the hill, trapping Reinhart. It wasn't permanent, but it would give us a head start. I looked ahead. A field spread out before us, but a few hundred yards away, the open land gave way to trees. Malcolm spurred the horse on, heading for the woodland. I gripped the shield and cloak tighter and held on to Malcolm, praying I wouldn't fall off, not daring to look until we reached the trees.

When we entered the forest, we slowed, and I looked over my shoulder. Reinhart and his men were halfway across the open land. The woods were not thick. They offered little concealment and no protection; all they did was slow us down. Reinhart would be only a hundred feet behind us when he reached the edge of the wood. I started to panic. Then

Malcolm drew the horse to a stop. I looked and saw that a deep ravine blocked our way.

"Dismount," Malcolm said. "Aelric and I will lead the horses to the other side. Meet us there."

I jumped from the horse. Charlie and I slid down into the ravine, scrambled up the other side and waited. As I watched the horses, led by Aelric and Malcolm, make their way nervously down the ravine, I used the time to put my shield on properly, bundle the cloak so I could carry it better, and watch. The horses skidded down the muddy slope, their eyes white with fear. At the bottom, they splashed across the stream, then began scaling the steep bank, their hooves slipping as they struggled to climb. And in the forest, the sounds of our pursuers grew louder.

When we were all at the top of the ravine, Malcolm went to mount his horse, but I pulled on his robe. "No," I said, "we need to stop."

Malcolm looked at me. Charlie and Aelric stopped and stared. None of them spoke.

"They're going to catch us," I continued. "You know that. There's nothing we can do about it."

Still, no one said anything.

I ran to the edge of the ravine. The sound of horse hooves and shouts grew louder. I looked down at the stream. Yes, it looked familiar.

"The Talisman showed this to me," I said, pointing into the crevice. "This is where we have to make our stand."

Malcolm smiled. "You learn well." He looked around, calculating. "We must be quick."

"Aelric," I said, "take the horses into the woods, out of sight, and tie them up."

"Then what?"

"Then come back and be ready."

"For what?" he asked, already leading the horses away.

I didn't answer him. "Charlie, help me cut some branches."

I looked around. Neither of us had a sword. I began pulling and twisting, then Malcolm produced a knife. It was short but sharp and made the job easier.

We hid our shields and the cloak, cut enough branches for us to hide behind, and settled in next to the edge of the ravine. Then I told Charlie and Malcolm what I had in mind.

"You think that will work?" Charlie asked.

"If the Talisman showed him, it will," Malcolm answered.

We said no more. Reinhart and his men had arrived at the far side of the ravine.

They hesitated only a moment before plunging down the side and splashing through the water. They had a harder time climbing up, but they shouted and cursed and—from the sounds of it—kicked their horses unmercifully to make them move. I waited, listening, watching, hoping. Then they appeared, clustered together, their heads, then the horse's heads, bodies, and long, sturdy legs. As soon as the four of them were on solid ground, but before they had moved away from the lip of the ravine, I turned to Charlie.

"Now!"

Charlie and I jumped up, waving our branches, rushing the horses, and shouting. Between us, not carrying the branches I had cut for him, was Malcolm, who raised his arms, holding his staff aloft, and looking more frightening than we did. It did the trick. The startled horses reared up and Reinhart, Gerwald,

259

Hoban and Blekwulf, still unsettled from the climb up the slope, fell. Malcolm rushed forward and grabbed two of the horses. Aelric appeared, seemingly from nowhere, and grabbed the other two.

Blekwulf and Hoban had fallen into the ravine—I heard them splashing and cursing—but Gerwald and Reinhart were lying next to the edge, and starting to get up. Charlie and I stopped and dropped our branches. Reinhart drew his sword. Gerwald had lost his axe, but he had a long and lethal-looking knife.

"Thought you could escape!" Reinhart thundered.

We could run, but they would catch us. And we had no weapons to face them with, not even our shields.

Then I heard hoof-beats, and a horse flashed between me and Charlie. On it was Aelric. He rode straight at Reinhart, who grinned and raised his sword. I thought Aelric was planning to run him down, throwing himself into the ravine as he did. I wanted to shout, "No," but at the last second, he pulled back on the reins and his horse went up on two legs. Reinhart ducked the flailing hooves, stepped back, and slipped over the edge. At the same moment, Malcolm ran up to Gerwald, swinging his staff. Gerwald stood his ground and took a hit in the head. He didn't fall into the ravine, but he dropped where he stood and didn't move.

"To the horses, quickly," Malcolm said.

We now had six horses. We each mounted one, and Malcolm and Aelric each led one of the spares.

"We must put as much distance between us and Reinhart as we can," Malcolm said. "They will not be without mounts for long, there are many riderless horses about."

The horses were distressed and tired, but we rode

until the light left the sky. Only then did we feel safe enough to stop. We camped near a stream, on the far side so we would hear if anyone came near. The horses drank and grazed, and we unsaddled them and took off their bridles. We knew they would need days to recover, but we didn't have time. We would need to ride again at first light.

Malcolm could have captured a rabbit, but we didn't dare light a fire, so we ate some berries that Aelric foraged while Malcolm was out gathering herbs. Then we drank from the stream and fell asleep on the grass.

Chapter 54

Charlie

I took the first turn on guard duty, scanning the open land for any signs of trouble. The stars were hidden behind clouds and, though every now and again a half moon would peek out, it was so dark, anyone more than ten feet away could walk right by and I wouldn't see them. That made me glad for the stream. At least if someone crept up on me, I'd hear them.

But it was quiet, deathly quiet. No wind, no animal noises, nothing, as if the land was in mourning. Then, far away, on the distant horizon, I saw a dim glow. And next to it, came another. A minute later, another glow, this one closer than the others, and with it came the faintest sounds of shouting and wailing. As I watched, I realized they were villages on fire.

We rose before dawn and headed west. Despite the lack of paths, Malcolm seemed to know where he was going. We trotted onward, moving faster as the sun rose higher. We rode over grass-covered downs, through forests, and passed villages—some destroyed and empty, others half-burnt, with the survivors still burying their dead and making repairs.

As we emerged from another strip of woodland, we saw a stone church on top of a small hill. Around it was nothing but a few burned out houses.

"This is the village of Worth," Aelric said, his voice

edged with alarm, as he looked at the devastation. "Or it was. William has destroyed it all. And Horsham is but ten miles away."

Without a word, he galloped off. I shouted after him, but Malcolm shook his head.

"Let him go. He needs to see if his wife and child are safe. We will catch up with him. But we must move on."

It took us an hour to get to Horsham. I held my breath as we came within sight, hoping, like Aelric, that it had been left intact. To my relief, it was still the same village of muddy streets, crooked houses, and powerful stench that we had come to know. Some villagers came out to watch as we rode past, but we didn't stop. We found the path to Aelric's house and soon saw him, standing next to Hilde, clutching Edric in his arms. To my amusement, I saw Hilde was wearing my sneakers.

We rode into the yard and dismounted. Hilde rushed to us, grabbing Mitch and me in a hug. "Thank you. Oh, thank you. You brought him home safe to me. It is a miracle."

Then Malcolm came forward, holding his staff. "Yes, a miracle, indeed. But it will not last." He swept his hand to the distant fields. "A darkness is coming on the Land. Gather what you can."

Aelric, still hugging Edric, looked at him. "What do you mean?"

"You must leave," Malcolm said. "At once." He handed the reins of his horse to Aelric. "Take this, and the others. We need only one."

Hilde, who seemed to understand the seriousness of the situation, ran into the house. She returned a minute later with a big bundle, dropped it at Aelric's feet and started to go back inside.

"Do you still have their clothing?" Malcolm asked her.

She stopped and blinked. "Yes. Yes, I do."

Malcolm looked at us. "We must hurry. We do not have much time."

We changed and helped Aelric and Hilde pack up their meagre belongings and tie them to the horses. I felt bad leaving Hilde shoe-less again, but she said she didn't mind.

Less than half an hour later, we rode from the farmyard, with Hilde and Edric on one horse, Aelric on another—leading a train of three horses behind him—and the three of us, Malcolm, Mitch, and me, on the remaining horse. We travelled on the road that led to the Roman villa, and the place where we had first met Pendragon. At the path that led to the field where we had appeared, we parted company.

"Go north," Malcolm said to Aelric. "As far as you can. Keep to the west, you will be safer there."

There was no time for hugs or handshakes, so we waved and rode off in separate directions.

As soon as we were on the narrow track, Malcolm pulled a leather bag from within his robe. Still riding, he managed to fill it with water. Then he shook it, twirled it, and looked inside.

"This would taste better if it was allowed to brew," he said, holding it behind his back so I could take it, "but we haven't the luxury of time. Drink half and give the rest to Mitch."

I put the sack to my lips and sucked it like it was a melted freezer pop. It was bitter and full of floating buds and almost made me gag. I drank what I could, then handed it to Mitch, who didn't like it any more than I did.

"What was that?" Mitch asked.

"My sleeping potion," Malcolm said. "It saved your brother's life once. Perhaps it will again."

We trotted at a fast clip, and soon I saw the field of cows with the bushes lining the border.

"This is it," I said. "Under there, near the edge."

We dismounted and headed for the spot. My legs felt heavy, and I gratefully flopped to the ground as soon as we reached the arrow, which was still in the ground. Mitch fell beside me. Malcolm took our shields and cloak from the horse's saddle bags and gave them to us. We put them on our chests and scooted under the low branches to as near the exact spot as we could. Then Malcolm spread the cloak over us.

"I must go now," Malcolm said. "Farewell."

I tried to tell him goodbye, but my tongue felt thick, and my words became garbled. Beside me, Mitch was already asleep. I closed my eyes and heard horses. Then I was dreaming, or floating. And in my dream, I saw Malcolm ride away. And from a different direction, I saw Reinhart, Gerwald, Hoban and Blekwulf arrive.

Gerwald pulled his horse to a halt. Reinhart and Blekwulf did the same.

"I heard a horse," Reinhart said. "They were here. They must be riding off."

Hoban scanned around him. I saw him look toward the bush we were under. "No," he said, pointing, "they are still here."

Gerwald jumped from his horse.

"I see their cloak," Blekwulf said. "It's there. They will not be far away."

"They are hiding beneath it," Reinhart said. "Like frightened women."

Gerwald pulled his axe from its holder and came

toward us.

"Kill them," Reinhart said.

Gerwald charged to where we lay, raging like a bull, raising his axe above his head. He brought the axe down, right where we were laying. Even though I wasn't there, and didn't have a body, I flinched.

But then I saw Gerwald look down. There was no blood, no severed heads, nothing but dry grass, moulded into the shape of two bodies, and his axe buried in the chalky earth.

Chapter 55
July 2015

Mitch

I opened my eyes. The familiar weight on my chest was gone. In the dark, my fingers felt the edges of the homemade shield granddad had sent. Beneath my back I felt a soft and warm mattress, not the hard ground. I nudged Charlie. "You awake?"

"Uh?"

I pulled the cloak off, sat up and waited for the room to stop spinning. Charlie sat up next to me, holding his head in his hands.

"What was in that stuff Malcolm fed us?"

Charlie glanced around the room as if he was surprised to see it. "We've been gone weeks," he said.

I looked at my bedside clock. "No, only for a few seconds. It's still the same time as when we left."

I got off the bed, still feeling shaky. "We better put this back where we found it before mom comes home," I said.

Charlie stood up next to me and started bundling the cloak. Then the front door opened and closed.

"Uh oh."

We waited, listening.

"She's just home early," Charlie said, trying to convince either himself or me, and failing on both counts. "She can't know—"

I heard a gentle squeak as the closet door opened.

"Please, no …"

Then came the sound of a zip being pulled. Seconds later, the door slammed, and heavy footsteps pounded up the stairs.

"Boys!"

We both sighed, sat back on the bed, and waited.

Historical Note

According to my (admittedly limited) research, the Battle of Stamford Bridge took place on an autumn day when the temperature reached 90 degrees F (32.2 C), which undoubtedly made the fighting even more gruelling.

By some accounts, Harold's race to York took only four days. It was, however, more likely at least a week. Still, for those times, that was unimaginably fast, and secured for Harold the element of surprise.

Though facing William with a depleted and fatigued army, the Battle of Hastings was a close run. Had Harold not been killed near the end of the fighting on the 14th of October 1066, there is every chance he could have eventually defeated the invading Normans.

Of course, had Mitch and Charlie not been delayed by two days, none of this would have happened. Harold would have remained on the throne, and Britain would not have been conquered by the Normans.

You can decide for yourself it that would have been a good thing or not.

About the Author

Michael Harling is originally from upstate New York. He moved to Britain in 2002 and currently lives in Sussex.

Lindenwald Press
Sussex, United Kingdom

Printed in Great Britain
by Amazon